L. J. Alexander was born in Poland in June 1985. She came to Ireland at the early age of 20 in 2006 and after discovering her true self, she made Dublin her home. In her successful and various careers, she always stayed true to her values and became an advocate for the LGBTQ+ community. Finally, in 2020, she could no longer ignore the writer within her and started working on her 1st book. This is her work of passion which she shares for writing and giving a voice to the LGBTQ+ community.

Special thanks to my beautiful partner for always cheering me on and believing that I can indeed finish this manuscript and much more, and to Austin Macaulay Publishers and the amazing team for picking this manuscript and believing in its success.

L. J. Alexander

IT WAS ALMOST PERFECT

AUSTIN MACAULEY PUBLISHERS™
LONDON * CAMBRIDGE * NEW YORK * SHARJAH

Copyright © L.J. Alexander 2023

The right of L.J. Alexander to be identified as author of this work has been asserted by the author in accordance with sections 77 and 78 of the Copyright, Designs and Patents Act 1988.

All rights reserved. No part of this publication may be reproduced, stored in a retrieval system, or transmitted in any form or by any means, electronic, mechanical, photocopying, recording, or otherwise, without the prior permission of the publishers.

Any person who commits any unauthorised act in relation to this publication may be liable to criminal prosecution and civil claims for damages.

This is a work of fiction. Names, characters, businesses, places, events, locales, and incidents are either the products of the author's imagination or used in a fictitious manner. Any resemblance to actual persons, living or dead, or actual events is purely coincidental.

A CIP catalogue record for this title is available from the British Library.

ISBN 9781398494985 (Paperback)
ISBN 9781398494992 (ePub e-book)

www.austinmacauley.com

First Published 2023
Austin Macauley Publishers Ltd®
1 Canada Square
Canary Wharf
London
E14 5AA

To all the amazing and supportive souls in my life, especially the ones that believed in me when I didn't believe in myself. To my mom for always believing I can be and do anything. To my amazing partner for all her support and patience and for being my number one fan. To my daughter who inspired me to be the best version of myself and follow my dreams so I can one day be the role model she deserves. To my long life and just starting friendships, and to everyone who touched my heart and inspired me to put the words on paper. And most of all, to my amazing grandmother who might not be here to read this, she is however always with me.

Alex

"So what brings you here?" Michelle asked with a soothing warmth in her voice.

Sun was bouncing of the sea across the street. Alex found herself distracted by the view behind her new therapist more than the question itself.

"It seems peaceful here," she replied.

"Thanks," Michelle smiled and prompted the question again. "So, Alex, what brings you to therapy?"

Alex took a deep, long breath as if the answer to that question carried a burden she didn't want to unravel. "See," she finally started, "I need to fix myself."

"Fix yourself how?"

"Fix myself so my partner of 7 years doesn't leave me," another long inhale followed. Alex closed her eyes, the pain and embarrassment she felt inside was clearly marked upon her face as the words left her lips.

"What would you like to fix?" Michelle asked.

"I don't really know, things, I guess. My partner thinks I should be on medication because I'm emotionally unstable. I'm angry, I blow up and apparently, I am quite miserable all the time."

"Is that how you feel?" Michelle shifted in her chair before she followed with another question. "What doesn't make you miserable?"

"I don't really know what I feel. I like going out for walks with my dog, and it makes me happy. I like to spend time with my friends, I'm after starting a new job, which is also quite exciting," slight smile crossed Alex's lips. Some glimpse of joy and happiness was uncovering in her previously sad eyes.

"I love the sea." Her focus was shifting to the outside world once again.

"It calms me down, it makes me happy."

"What else do you like? What else makes you happy?"

"Everything and anything really." Alex took a breath before she blurred out a tone of words. "Sun, my dog, music, coffee, definitely coffee, good book, self-improvement pod cast, cooking, sea, long walks in nature, going to town for a wonder, talking to my friends."

Michelle smiled as Alex's back straighten and a big smile was now visible on her face, her eyes glowing with relief, her body language changed, and she was fully relaxed. "I also got a new job, as a regional manager," she continued. "I love what I do and the company I work for. I have met a lot of new people who really believe in me. It's amazing how other people believing in you can help your self-esteem."

"So, you can list all these things that make you happy? Yet you told me you are miserable. So, tell me," Michelle continued, "what makes you unhappy?"

Alex's body fell back into the chair, the big smile went away and the glow in her eyes disappeared.

"Fights." She was now looking at Michelle as if the beautiful view outside the window didn't exist. "Fights with my partner make me unhappy, I go so low when we fight, I say and do things I don't want to say. It's like it's not even me. I don't know myself anymore."

"OK, and why do you think you need medication."

"I don't think I do." Alex was unsure of what she thinks or what the truth is anymore. "I think I'm OK, I think I react to the situation I am put in. I mean I am OK anywhere else you know? I am just unhappy at home, ironically the place that should make me the happiest, the safest."

"If you don't think you need medication, why do you let someone else's voice be louder than yours?" Michell's words cut Alex deeper than a sharp knife; they really got to the core of what she was afraid of. They were the pathway to the truth she was not ready for yet.

"This isn't your first therapy?" Michelle's voice broke the silence.

"No," Alex replied. "My partner asked me to go to a new therapist as the old one wasn't helping. I mean she helped me a lot, she was great, and I was really happy with the progress and healing I got from it. It's just," Alex took a break gasping for air.

"You OK?"

"Yes, it's just Niamh doesn't think I made any progress, she is still unhappy with the way I am."

"Niamh? Is that your partner's name?"

"Yes, we are together seven years and I am really doing my best to figure this thing out."

"What do you think you should do?"

"I don't know. I am trying all that I can, but it never seems to be enough. We have separated twice earlier this year and we are giving it another go. You commit to someone and put 7 years into a relationship, I think it's worth few more months, you know just to try."

"You must do whatever feels right, either way it's not easy. Any decision will be hard in this situation." Michelle smiled as she looked at the clock.

"I'm afraid our time is up for today."

"OK, thanks," said Alex. "Can I just ask. Do you think I need medication?" Michelle smiled.

"I will just repeat this, why do you let someone else's voice be louder than yours? What do you think?"

"I think, no."

"Then you need to learn to trust yourself."

45 minutes went very fast. Alex was relieved the first session was behind her but the answers she was looking for over the past 4 years didn't come today. Maybe next time, she thought to herself as she left the building.

She went outside and crossed the street to have a look at the sea. The tide was in and the sun rays danced on top of the water's surface. She sat down on the bench and closed her eyes, she looked up to feel the sun on her face.

She was happy. She was relieved and had a little more strength then before. Tomorrow is another day, she thought to herself as she stood up to walk back home.

Noelle

Sun was shining through the window as she woke to a smell of freshly brewed coffee.

"Breakfast is ready," call came from downstairs.

Noelle smiled to herself as she pulled off the sheets. She went to the bathroom, looked at the slight wrinkles around her eyes. Only a couple of months till 40. She never really cared about age, she was young at heart and in an amazing shape. This one, this one was different.

40, what a number. She always considered herself very lucky, blessed even. Amazing home, beautiful car, successful career and a loving husband. A man by her side who loved and adored her for the past 15 years. Their anniversary was coming up and they were planning a holiday to celebrate.

She had it all and she knew it. Anything any girl could ever want. Yet sometimes, inside, she felt empty. She put a silk robe on her naked body and a smile on her face and went downstairs to a table full of freshly made food and cup of the best coffee money can buy. She kissed her husband on the cheek.

"Thank you," she smiled. "This looks amazing."

"Anything for you," he smiled back as he pushed the plate towards her. "Everything OK? You look upset."

"No, no I am only after waking up, you know it takes me awhile."

She glanced at the table, full of fresh pastries and colourful fruit and freshly cut flowers from their garden. She knew how hard he always tried to make her happy, to be there for her, to do anything she wants. She appreciated all his effort yet didn't really feel what she thought she should feel, what she was supposed to feel.

He even took care of school runs and play dates for their two kids. He was an amazing dad and a great guy, and most of her friends have always been jealous of the strong bond and relationship they had.

"You know how much I love you," he whispered into her ear while putting his shoulders around her in a warm embrace.

"I know," she replied.

"Kids are at my mum's," he whispered. "Would you like to, I don't know, go back upstairs for a while?" His lips pressed against the skin on her neck. "You smell so good."

"Can we leave it for later?" she asked as she pulled away towards the table. "I'm sorry I have so much to do for my meeting on Monday morning, and we have some new staff coming down for training. I feel distracted."

"Yes, of course," he replied trying to cover his disappointment with a smile. "Whatever you want."

She knew it became quite a routine, she didn't feel like or didn't want to be intimate. The stress of work and raising two kids, the feeling of missing out on something. She wasn't quite sure how can you miss something you never had, while she had everything anyone could ever want.

They finished the rest of the breakfast in silence and both got on with their days. Dishes, laundry cleaning and collecting kids won't do itself.

It must have been 2 hours later, when Noelle looked out the window as Liam went out to the car to drive to his mum for early lunch and to collect the twins. She must have dosed off as she didn't know where the time went. She sat at the table and opened her PC.

"OK Monday," she said out loud with a cheeky smile as if she was daring someone. "Tomorrow, I am going to kick your ass," she whispered as she opened her mailbox.

Gabriela

It was exactly a year since she came over to this amazing country to fulfil her dreams and live a better life. Sun was shining and even with a cool breeze coming from the river it was still extremely warm. Dublin warm, not Brazil warm. She just finished her shift and grabbed a coffee on the way out.

She went to her favourite spot near the bridge and opened the book she was so eager to finish. *The Secret* was going to give her all the answers and all the tools she needed to get the life she wanted. She dived into the pages as she sipped her coffee, and this was all she needed to make this day special.

It must have been an hour later when her phone buzzed quite loudly. Gabriela's friend's determination to take her out so she can expand her social circle was quite impressive. Although, she never really wanted to do much after finishing work they never stopped trying.

"Can you please help me out tonight as my ass of a sister stood me out."

Even though the text sounded quite desperate, she still didn't want to participate.

"Please, you are literally the last person I can ask, and I really don't want these tickets to go to waste"

As tempting as an idea of a mysterious pair of tickets was, she already had her ideal day planned and didn't want anything to interrupt it. She read the text again and looked at the book lying on her lap. Maybe just maybe it's the universe's way to get her out of her comfort zone.

I will open the book and let it guide me, she thought to herself quite delighted with her playful new way of deciding on what clearly was a matter of life and death.

'The secret to the world' was the heading on the page she opened.

'Anything we focus on we create' were the words that caught her eyes. I can't create anything in my life unless I get to experience life, she thought to herself as she took last sip of what was now a cold coffee. I guess that's it then,

I'm going to do something different today. She looked up at the blue sky. There, universe, I hope your happy.

"What time should I meet you and where?" She replied.

"OMG, you are the best," the reply came quite quickly.

"I will collect you at 8:30, dress sharp, we are going to a gallery." Couple of fancy emojis with martini glasses and men in tuxedos followed.

We are going to a what now? Well that's just great, she thought. I don't like drinking, I don't appreciate art and now I must make myself suitably dressed and endure both. Man, what an evening this is going to be. *The Secret* has spoken, she wanted more for herself and her life and knew she needs to get out and find things to enjoy.

She just wasn't sure if she should try and do things that she found enjoyable or enjoy things that other people enjoyed. This life mystery was not quite clear to her.

She went home and opened her wardrobe.

"What in the world am I going to wear?" she said out loud hopelessly searching through all the clothes she had, at the end she picked a fitted grey suit pants and a black blouse. That seemed like a suitable outfit for the occasion.

She found a bottle of red wine under her roommates' bed and poured herself a glass. A cup actually, she couldn't find any wine glasses in the apartment. How does one not have a wine glass, she laughed at the thought of a Brazilian student, barista living in a house without wine glasses going to an art gallery for a Sunday night entertainment.

I am just going to make a great conversation partner, she was cracking herself up picturing the hopeless evening she was about to experience. Deep down, she felt curious and even a little excited.

Car pulled outside the apartment at 8:30 pm sharp. Gabriela just finished doing her hair and makeup. She wasn't sure if it was the wine or the feeling of the unknown that was awaiting her downstairs, but she started to feel a little…happy. One last look in the mirror, she was quite pleased with herself. She glanced at the book left on her bed side locker as she was leaving the bedroom.

"You better not let me down," she whispered as she closed the door.

Alex

The door opened and Michelle's smiley face popped out. "Come in," she said somewhat happy and surprised to see Alex back.

"Hi," said Alex in a much more relaxed manner than last week.

"Hi," Michelle responded. "How are you?"

"I'm good, great actually."

"OK, great, would you like to share anything?" Michelle asked playfully.

"I had a fantastic week, focused on walks and gym. Just looking after myself you know. Work is going great. I really like to meet new people and challenge myself and I'm doing well."

"Great," Michelle seemed genuinely happy with her patients improved attitude. "And how is everything at home?"

"Yea, it's fine." Alex replied a little less eagerly. "I mean we didn't fight this week, I started expressing my needs and our communication is better." Her body lifelessly fell into the chair.

"Tell me more about your work."

"Work is really good, I'm working there a couple of months but making amazing progress." Alex was once again eager to talk as her energy seemed to increase.

"It's a green, organic company with products known all over Europe, I really like their message and commitment to the safe and healthy environment. I'm so happy I came across this opportunity."

"Can you see the difference?" Michelle interrupted.

"The difference?" Alex asked confused.

"The difference in your response, body language," she explained. "You are full of energy and optimism, your body lifts of the chair but when I ask you about your home or relationship."

"Everything is OK, I mean it's better."

"That's what your words say, not your body language." Alex could lie to herself but she failed to deceive her new therapist.

"What do you see for yourself in the future when it comes to your relationship?" Michelle asked.

"Honestly, I'm not sure."

"OK, let's try an exercise. Close your eyes and imagine it's your 25-year anniversary. What do you want to say when you raise a toast?" Alex's body shivered, fear spread across her face.

"Are you OK?" Michelle asked concerned as she has rarely seen such a strong physical reaction.

"Yes, I'm OK." Alex reached for a glass of water to clear her throat. "I felt like a massive weight fell on me and spread across my chest. I couldn't breathe there for a second."

"Is this because of my question?" Michelle asked in a calm voice.

"I don't know." Alex wasn't sure what was happening, she was battling questioning her relationship for so long. "I imagine how things should be, drive home on a Friday evening and I am so looking forward to starting a weekend. Then I go home and within 10 minutes we are arguing over something, it always escalates to the point we don't even know why we started but now we rehash things from 5 years ago. Things that don't really matter anymore. And it's always my fault."

"Why is that?" Michelle asked.

"Well, that's what I'm told anyway. Doesn't matter how I say or do something it feels like I can't do it right. There is always something Niamh questions or…"

"Or?"

"Or has a problem with." Alex took a minute to gather her thoughts. "I am not an angel and never try to make myself look like one. I blow up, I put myself in situations that are borderline wrong."

"Like what?" Michelle felt they were making progress.

"Like drinking a little too much and maybe becoming a little flirtatious. I don't know. I want to feel desired, I guess. Wanted."

"You don't feel desired by your partner?"

"Well, I don't know she tells me not to be too confident, that my confidence is not attractive and…" Alex seemed embarrassed.

"It's OK. This is a safe space." Michelle comforted her with a gentle smile.

"Well, our sex life is pretty much not existing. I want to feel more, be more."

"OK, let's try this again. Close your eyes and tell me what do you see in your future?"

Alex closed her eyes but all she could see is darkness. "I don't really see anything."

"What would you like to see in your future? Or rather what would you like your future to be."

Alex smiled as she closed her eyes again. That was clear to her.

"I see myself happy, joyful and fulfilled. I am meditating daily, I read books and enjoy fitness, gym and walks on the beach and I guess I am with someone who is like me and who is enjoying the same things."

As she finished the sentence, their time was up. Still there was no answer to the questions she carried like a weight on her shoulders. With each session, however, she was getting stronger and the vision of what she wants her life to be clearer.

Noelle

The week was long, it felt like it is never going to end. Nonetheless, it was behind her and she was happy to swap her 6-inch heels for her weekend attire. Trainers and gym leggings were her favourite. As she cuddled on the couch with her 8-year-old kids to indulge in another magical Disney moment she looked around the room.

The beautiful wooden floors, the large open plan kitchen and state of the art home cinema. She was proud of the comforts she was able to provide for her family, as a child growing up in a country, she was never able to dream about a fraction of the things her boys treated as a normality. She looked at Liam sitting in the armchair across from her, his reading glasses on and boyish good looks reminded her why she fell for him.

From all the guys chasing after her she went for the most gentle, caring and loving guy you could ever meet. His patience and devotion to his family was out of this world. He never lost his temper or even got slightly agitated when the kids misbehaved. He always seemed to know what to say or do.

Sometimes, only sometimes she wished he would lose it. So, she would feel less guilty for losing her temper. Sometimes she got frustrated and didn't know how to handle work, kids, home. Sometimes she felt like a prisoner. Prisoner locked up in the most beautiful home and life possible.

She loved her kids deeply and respected her husband, yet even in this most beautiful evening she felt somehow out of place. She looked around the room again. Her home was amazing, two healthy boys, loving husband. Why couldn't she feel more joy? What was wrong with her?

Those questions often came to her mind. Work was busy, work was taking all her strength. Work was stressful. Having a glass or two of wine in the evening helped in soothing her mind. The guilt would come and go, she could think about picture perfect Christmas mornings during which she was happy for her kids and family yet absent.

She felt like an observer of the most amazing moments but couldn't make herself feel what she was supposed to. What was she supposed to feel anyway? They don't teach this in any class, she tried looking for one. She felt like she had to be so many things for so many people.

She had to be a loving and devoted wife, nurturing mum, a career woman, fair but firm boss. And the appearance. Trips to hairdressers, beauty salon and daily gym routine. All to make herself fit in this picture-perfect family. She did it all so good.

But between all those activities and titles and expectations, she lost a part of herself, a sense of who she is. Somehow, she knew she had more to experience, more to discover. The thought of her 40th birthday was scaring her, such a milestone and in some ways a gateway to the last part of her life.

Yet she felt like there is so much more she wanted to do. So much more she wanted to learn about herself. The movie has ended, and it took Noelle about 10 minutes to realise the boys were asleep on top of her and Liam was still reading his book. She was so deep in thought, it took her another 10 minutes before she got up.

"Oh, it's over." Liam looked up from behind the book cover.

"It is," Noelle replied.

"I will take them up." Liam gave her a kiss on the cheek as he picked up two sleepy heads. "You just relax and pour yourself a glass of wine. You deserve it after the week you had, I will see you upstairs in a while?" He asked as he walked towards the stairs. The boys carried by their dad didn't even flinch from their deep sleep.

"I just might," said Noelle with a smile on her face as she walked towards the fridge. She emptied the last of the red wine into the glass. Did he not even notice I already had 2 glasses? She thought to herself, sometimes she felt invincible.

She opened her laptop to make sure all the tasks form the week were done. She often went back to work after everyone was asleep. It was her favourite time of the day. So much peace, so quiet, no phone calls or emails coming in. That's weird, she thought to herself as an email hit her mailbox, she didn't know the sender. Who would be mailing her at 22:20 on a Friday night?

Weekly report from Ola Kucharczyk.

She will definitely get to the bottom of this mysterious sender on Monday, more so because of the impressive predictions of sale figures and new supply chains she was looking at. If this is a new weekly thing, she could get used to it. She opened her own company when she was 20 and devoted every ounce of time and energy until she build her name up to be a globally well-known brand.

She was hard working and she loved people who also worked hard. She felt a spark of excitement she didn't feel in a long time. After she finished reading the report, her curiosity went on to the sender.

She was one of the new of employees, in the company only few months but already making some impressive progress even in the eastern European markets Noelle was trying to get into for so long.

So, who are you miss Kucharczyk, she thought to herself as she went on to her linked in profile.

"Well that's impressive," Noelle said out loud as she devoured all the information on the page.

The curiosity didn't stop there. She put her name into Google, no Facebook account, no twitter finally, Instagram. "And bingo." Noelle realised she said it a little too loud. Hopefully, she didn't wake anyone. She looked at her empty glass of wine.

I think this calls for a top up. She opened another bottle and poured a hefty portion. Cute dog, she thought as she went through some of the pictures.

It was 2 am before Noelle realised, she is now sort of stalking her new employee. She felt a little bad for such an invasion of privacy and a little excited for Monday morning.

Gabriela

The doors of the taxi opened, and Gabriela found herself standing in front of an impressive looking gallery.

"You cannot be serious?" she said to her friend.

"Ah come, it will be fun," Bruna answered cheerfully.

"Why are we even here?" Gabriela demanded some explanation before she threw herself completely into this uncharted territory.

"Well, there is this guy at work."

"Your messing?" Gabriela rolled her eyes, "a guy?"

"Well he might be here and I really wanted to meet him like randomly," Bruna gave her one of those innocent smiles.

"OK," Gabriela was having none of it. "So we go in, you will 'randomly' come across the guy form work and I will be left on my own for the evening?"

"I won't leave you," Bruna tried to sound convincing but they both knew sooner or later this was bound to happen.

"OK, I will go in," said Gabriela. "But only because *The Secret* told me so."

"The who?" Bruna gave her a confused look.

"Doesn't matter, let's go and don't make me regret this."

They walked towards the gallery on cobble stones, Bruna's heels got stuck about five times to Gabriela's entertainment. At least that's funny, she thought to herself. As they approached the door a very well dressed man opened it for them.

"I am able to open my own door; thank you very much," said Gabriela in disbelief.

"My friend is joking, thank you," said Bruna as she pushed Gabriela inside. "That's his job, you are in a civilised world now, please behave."

Gabriela felt rather silly not realising a gallery like this on a big event would have a door man service. Of course they would have a door man service. I really need to get out more, she thought to herself.

Tickets checked, jackets in a cloak room and glass of red wine in her hand she felt much better now. Bruna was eagerly looking around like a little lost puppy.

"Relax girl, you are not leaving me remember."

"Oh I know, sorry, it's just I really, really like him." Bruna's eyes had that dreamy look.

"Wow, you are so hopeless."

"Just because you never met anyone you like doesn't mean we all have to die virgins."

"Excuse me?" Gabriela was not one bit impressed with that comment.

"You know what I mean."

An hour and two glasses of wine later, Gabriela hopelessly followed Bruna from one room into another, sculptures, paintings they all looked the same. They entered another room, somehow it was different. Full of beautiful pictures, nature and native forgotten tribes from all over the world.

It was innocent, mysterious and fascinating. Gabriela wasn't sure if it's the wine or did she actually start to enjoy her evening even though until now it seemed like an episode of amazing race.

"There he is," Bruna pointed at some guy in the corner smiling at her.

"There you go so," Gabriela knew she's on her own.

"Come, I will introduce you." Bruna wasn't even looking at her anymore; her puppy eyes said it all.

"It's OK, you go and have fun I will wander here for a while and head home soon if you don't need me." Gabriela smiled at Bruna

"Thank you!" Bruna whispered and off she went ready for her adventure.

Gabriela was thankful she was left alone in this magical room. She loved every picture, she wanted to explore and enjoy the beauty without having to pursue some stranger her friend was hung up on. She wanted to know the story behind each face.

"What do you see?" Gabriela heard a female voice coming from behind her, she didn't answer as she didn't think the question was directed at her.

"In the pictures, what do you see in the pictures?" This time she turned around, a tall brunette with caramel skin and almond shaped eyes stood behind her smiling,

"Me?" Gabriela asked in disbelief.

"I don't see anyone else," said the stranger in a deep voice with a soft American accent. Gabriela laughed nervously, the wine really got to her head. Maybe it wasn't the wine, maybe it was the strong scent of perfume from this beautiful nearly goddess like woman. Sweet, sort of musky scent.

"I…" she got a little embarrassed and a little nervous. "I think they are beautiful," she finally blurred out some words. "I don't know much about art," she continued. "But they are innocent, pure, mysterious."

She was pretty proud of herself being able to get all of that out while drowning in the depth of the stranger's eyes.

"Pretty accurate, I'm Karina." Gabriela looked at the pictures, Karina Ferrer was the name written at the bottom of each one. She quickly made a connection, she was glad even after a few glasses of wine she still had her wits about her.

"You're the author?" she asked.

"I'm the photographer," said Karina. "And who are you?"

"My name is Gabriela. I'm here with a friend but she…" Gabriela threw a quick glance around the room knowing well her friend is no longer here. "She met her prince charming and is probably on the way to his castle." Karina laughed loudly.

"You're funny, I like that. Well, Gabriela, what brings you here? All I normally get is pretentious, privileged art connoisseurs who are looking to bring a little bit of culture into their homes, not cute girls like you."

"Well, Karina," Gabriela didn't believe her bravery on the outside while inside she was now shaking like a little helpless puppy. "I am here to save you from those pretentious people." A sudden rush of warmth took over her body as the words left the tip of her tongue, she could feel herself blush. Karina laughed again, her voice was so warm and deep nearly as deep as her black eyes.

They sat down in the corner on a beautiful leather sofa and talked for what seemed like eternity. They laughed, they joked and Gabriela felt as if she knew her for years, like somehow they have met before.

"Here you are," a man's voice sounded relieved. "Karina, the buyers are waiting to talk to you."

"I'm really sorry." Karina looked at Gabriela. "Looks like your saving came to its end, I do appreciate the effort." She kissed Gabriela on the cheek and slipped something into her hand.

Gabriela wasn't able to stand up, she wasn't sure if it was the wine or the perfume that overwhelmed her and took away her ability to walk. Karina threw her a quick glance before she disappeared in the crowd.

Sometime later, Gabriela got the strength to walk out of the gallery. Still slightly light headed, she walked all the way to her apartment, taking in every street, every building, every shape and colour as if her senses somehow sharpened. She saw beauty in places she didn't even look at before.

While she walked, the conversation played over and over in her head. Especially the last part. She was holding on to a little piece of paper in her hand and the words, 'Call me, lets grab a coffee' written on the back. She looked at Karina's card and phone number in disbelief.

Alex

The past two Sundays were pretty good, Alex was able to get some time for herself and stay with her thoughts and try to figure out what is it that she wants or needs from her partner, her career, her life and what she needs to allow herself to do. Who she wants to be.

She was looking forward to her 3rd session; she felt the time she spend in therapy was the only time she has for herself. She allowed herself to have an hour a week with no distractions or no one wanting anything. No phone calls, no house chores, no inside or outside voices just her in those four walls with a beautiful view outside the window and a person who was not judging her.

She always felt judged, growing up being a tomboy in a society full of feminine women, she didn't quite fit and she knew it, so she left and made Dublin her home at an early stage of her life and never looked back. Her mind was drifting to the times when she had to make difficult decisions and how they changed the course of her life. Michelle moved around in her chair.

"So, how are you today?" she asked with a subtle smile.

"I'm great." Alex smiled a very hopeful and happy smile for the first time in three weeks.

"Great, tell me about your week."

"Work is amazing, I'm learning so much and meeting so many people I can't believe the progress I'm making in just few months." Her smile shined even brighter. "I really feel lucky like I got to the right place at the right time."

"That sounds fantastic." Michelle was really happy to hear the enthusiasm in her clients voice. "And how is everything else," she continued.

"I joined a gym, you know for once I decided I really want to do something that I love. Give myself some time and not always look after needs of others."

"You want to tell me more about that." Michelle made a note in her notebook. "The looking after needs of others part?"

"Well, you know we get into a relationship and I guess forget who we are. I always supported my partner, moved around when her work needed her to transfer, took care of the house and dropped her to work, often collected her after. My previous job was flexible so I always made sure I looked after her needs."

"You supported your partner, that's what a good relationship is right?" Michelle asked.

"Yea, I guess to some point, not to the point where you neglect yourself, neglect and lose your friends, don't really see your family."

"How do you feel about taking some time back for yourself?"

"It feels great." Alex smiled. "Don't get me wrong, I did all that to myself, for years I put other people first and it got to the point where it was expected, and I did that no one has done it to me."

"Interesting." Michelle once again wrote something. "So what's next?"

"I don't know," Alex still wasn't sure about the future. "It's nice you know, to take some time back, bit by bit look after myself. New job, new opportunities, new people," she smiled a little too enthusiastically.

"New people?"

"Yes, I met someone. I mean I meet a lot of people you know new job but last week I met someone and we sort of clicked."

"Tell me more." Michelle shifted in her chair and leaned towards Alex.

"I don't know, it's nothing, as I said I meet a lot of people lately but last week, I made a sort of connection with someone. It's probably all in my head but I felt like she was flirting with me and it just made me feel good you know, noticed."

"That's normal, in a long term relationships we sometimes enjoy an innocent encounter with a stranger, what happened?"

"Nothing really, we chatted and grabbed a coffee and chatted some more and that's it. The week ended, I went out on Friday and after few drinks, I couldn't get her out of my head. Imagined how it would feel to be out together and dance, maybe something more but I felt stupid and guilty. I stopped. I'm with someone else and again it's all in my head."

"Close your eyes." Alex listened as the last time the exercise proved pretty powerful. "Now imagine a bus; the bus is full of different people all of them are parts of your personality, who do you see?"

"I see happiness, joy, and I guess guilt sitting in the corner, and this other guy just lurking from the back, you know the voice that tells you that things are annoying." Both Michelle and Alex laughed. "That guy is in the back thought." Alex continued, "He sorts of just keeps moaning to himself."

"Is it noisy or quiet?"

"It's quite noisy." Alex's eyes remained closed. "It's very noisy, there is all sort of shouting across to each other."

"OK, and who is driving the bus? What part of you is driving?"

Alex had to think for a while and really focus on that one. She had to dig deep and quiet all the voices and characters in her head. She looked around and as she went pass every one of them she finally got a glimpse at the driver.

"Curiosity, the driver is curious. She is eagerly looking around enjoying the road; she likes to discover different things, learn."

"She is hungry for life," Michelle smiled. "You, Alex, have an appetite for life."

Alex left the appointment few minutes later. Every week, it seemed to go so fast. She wanted it to last longer but at the same time she was only able to unravel things slowly. Like a big puzzle she was able to put one piece at the time.

She stepped out on the path; sun was shining and water was shimmering on the other side of the street just like when she came here for the first time. This time, she was smiling to herself. She was happy; she was hopeful for the future and so much clearer on what she wants and needs to do.

Noelle

Noelle woke before the alarm went off, eagerly took a shower and picked her best dress for this Monday morning. She couldn't understand why she was so happy and excited about this day. Her new employee was making a lot of progress which would eventually bring in a lot of profit, she thought that must be the reason for her eagerness.

She never felt this way before meeting anyone, and at the end of the day she was the boss, she had all the power, yet she felt like a little girl going to school for the first time, she was both excited and nervous. The feeling was quite foreign to her but she enjoyed the anticipation. She kissed the boys and Liam and wished everyone a great day, hopped into her brand new black Mercedes and picked up a coffee on the way in from a little cute café across the street.

The girl who served her had dreamy eyes and brown curly hair flawlessly falling down on her shoulders. She never noticed her before. They exchanged some pleasantries and moved on with their day. The office was quite empty Noelle realised, she was there early, earlier than usual and so was Ola.

She sends emails last thing on Friday evening and shows up before anyone else on a Monday morning, interesting, Noelle thought to herself, trying to figure out how to approach her and start the conversation. She didn't want to come on too strong or come across weird. She was a little nervous which was hard for her to understand as she was known for her nerves of steel. Ola was standing by the coffee pot waiting for it to fill up.

"There is a little café across the street." Ola looked around and realised Noelle is talking to her as there was no one else in the office

"Thank you, I will remember that," she replied.

"Just in case you are not in the mood to wait for it here." Noelle knew that sounded lame but she didn't want the conversation to end too quickly. She was intrigued by the new girl and wanted to know more about her before she realised she was talking to the boss. "Can't start a week without a coffee," she continued as she took a sip from her take away cup.

"You know you can get one of those 'cups for life' in there," Ola said playfully. "Working for a green company and all we should be setting an example." Noelle laughed as she realised she is using a non-recyclable cup in a place where everything is green and good for the environment. She wanted to play this game a little longer but she could not let the opportunity pass.

"You would think I would know considering I started this green business before anyone ever cared for the planet," she pointed at the picture of herself in the office across from where they were standing. Ola's face went red. In a cute kind of way, she smiled a shy and embarrassed smile showing off her dimples.

"I'm so sorry I didn't realise."

"It's OK," said Noelle laughing.

"I'm…"

"Ola," Noelle's face was now covered with a little cheeky smile. "I know, I got your email on Friday evening."

"I'm so sorry to email you so late, I didn't think you will see it till Monday."

"No, no, it's fine. You apologise a lot, don't you." Noelle felt she is in control, she no longer felt like a little girl, she was the strong independent woman she knew. "Those Prediction figures are impressive; maybe you can tell me how have you done so much in so little time."

She was down to business now, she didn't want the conversation to get here so quickly but she was just going with it.

"Well, maybe we can chat over a coffee in that little café you told me about." Ola was surprisingly ballsy for someone who just moments ago didn't realise they were talking to their boss. "Unless you're busy."

"No, that sounds good," Noelle smiled. "A coffee meeting, I like that. Let me check my schedule and I will reply to your mail in a while."

"Sounds great. I really wanted to take you through some ideas just didn't want to approach you without someone introducing us." Ola smiled, she seemed much more relaxed now.

"That sounds great. I'm looking forward to it. Looks like your coffee is ready," Noelle pointed at the pot. "I better go and get rid of this filthy non-recyclable cup before anyone else sees it."

"That's wise," Ola smiled. She was always quite relaxed meeting new people but this time she wasn't sure where the boundary is and she didn't want to come across non-professional in the eyes of her boss. "One more thing though, everyone calls me Alex. Ola is a polish version, I prefer the, let's call it, western one."

"Alex it is." Noelle smiled and went into her office.

The week went quite quickly for both of them and Monday coffee meting turned into a coffee each day. They chatted about the business, new ideas and opportunities. Noelle was very pleased with the progress they made and started making some changes in her business plan for the next year.

She felt comfortable around Alex. She normally doesn't feel that around people she just met, even old time friends. She couldn't believe it's already Friday; she was happy it's the weekend but at the same time she didn't want to walk out of the office, it would mean she won't see Alex for two days.

But why does she want to see her? The confusion made her feel uneasy but also excited. She opened IM and looked for Alex's name.

"Hi"

"Hi" Message popped on her screen within seconds.

"Thanks for a great week and the fresh eye. I think we can make a great progress over the next while."

"No problem." Alex replied. "I'm really happy I can bring some new perspective."

"You sure have ☺" Noelle thought for a while before she continued. "Right, go and enjoy your weekend."

"Thank you ☺" Alex was still typing; Noelle was waiting for the next IM with anticipation.

"Here is my number. I'll be out this evening; if you're around town drop me a text."

Noelle turned her IM to offline. She didn't know what to reply. Her heart was beating a little stronger and the palms of her hands were sweating. Surely Alex meant it in a friendly way. It must be a friendly proposal, they felt very comfortable around each other.

It must have been a friendly text. Noelle thought as she left the office, she drove home and found herself sitting in the car for a while before she went into the house to greet her 3 boys.

Gabriela

Weeks went by but Gabriela couldn't shift the mysterious stranger out of her mind. She would come home each day after work and lie on the bed with a joint in one hand and Karina's business card in the other. She would play the conversation over and over in her head.

At this point, she was forgetting the sound of her voice and how her face looked in the shimmering candle lights of the gallery. She found herself upset thinking that one day she will completely forget the strangers smile. As crazy as it sounded, she knew she has to see her again.

Her heart was pounding every time she was brave enough to think about picking up the phone and actually taking her up on the coffee offer. She wouldn't have said it if she didn't mean it? Or would she? The questions on Gabriela's mind were relentless. She was exhausted at this point and decided she needs some divine intervention to make this call.

"Now, 'Secret', you didn't let me down before don't do it now," she said out loud as she reached for the book lying on her bed side table. She closed her eyes and took few deep breaths. "Should I or should I not be crazy enough to reach out to this perfect beautiful stranger I met once in my life yet can't stop thinking about," with some amount on anticipation Gabriela opened the book at random.

'The Secret to Relationships' was the heading on the page. This is utterly crazy, Gabriela thought to herself, none the less *The Secret* has spoken once again. Relationship is a strong word, my friend, she continued her train of thoughts; but if that's not a sign I don't know what is.

Gabriela smiled to herself and picked up the phone. She slowly typed in the mobile digits from the card and nervously listened to each and every sound on the other side of the line. One, two, three, four beeps and nothing she was ready to hung up when she heard a voice, a voice she only heard once before yet it sounded so familiar.

"Hello," the accent she remembered so well.

"Hi, it's me." Gabriela realised how ridiculous that sounded, as if she remembers who I am.

"Let me start over, we met two weeks ago in the gallery I was looking at your pictures."

"Oh, Hi. If you are interested in buying, you can just ring the gallery tomorrow morning. I will be happy to meet you and go over any pieces you are interested in."

Pictures, art, exhibition, now it was all clear to her. Karina is an artist, she takes pictures, puts them in frames, hangs them up on the walls so people can admire her work, fall in love, and buy them. And she gave me her number so I can do the same, not to ring her on a Friday evening hoping for what? Gabriela's head was spinning, her heart stopped.

"What was I thinking?" She said nearly out loud before she continued.

"No, I don't want to buy anything, I mean I loved your pictures, but I just rang to say Hi." Not very smooth, Gabriela felt like a complete fool. "You don't remember me?" Karina didn't answer.

"We sat on the sofa and talked." When she finished the sentence, she realised how ridiculous and desperate she sounded. That brief conversation on the couch didn't make her special.

"I remember," Karina replied after a while. It seemed to Gabriela she was enjoying hearing her scramble, nonetheless it brought a sense of relief to Gabriela's mind, her heart calmed down.

"It took you a while to call me."

"I was looking for a reason."

"OK, what is it then? What's the reason?" Karina's voice was seductive, deep, and raspy. Gabriela felt she can lose control and any senses she had left very easily.

"Well." Gabriela was struggling. "Honestly, I didn't find one." She could hear Karina laugh on the other side of the phone; an overwhelming feeling of desire was taking over her body. She felt shivers down her spine she wasn't sure how to handle it.

She would never believe what was going to happen next.

"You want to come over then?" She wasn't sure was it a question or an invitation; it made Gabriela speechless, which was not a rare sight. All she hoped for was a coffee date and a conversation, all she hoped for was to see that face and those eyes one more time.

"Are you there?" Karina asked. "Your call; take it or leave it."

"I'll be there in 20 minutes, just give me the address."

Gabriela checked herself in the mirror before she left the apartment. She threw on skinny jeans and a black fitted shirt buttoned all the way to the top. She brushed her curly brown hair and put on some eye liner to bring out the hazel in her eyes.

She run out of the house and hopped in a taxi waiting outside. She didn't know what to expect but she recognised the address. The apartment was located just by the river, the taxi brought her outside of the new exclusive building. She typed in the code at the front door and got into the elevator which brought her to the very top floor.

Her heart was pounding and she could hear her own pulse in her ears. As if hundred galloping horses were running through her veins. She regretted the choice of her outfit as sweat was pouring down at the back of her neck. The elevator door opened, Gabriela slowly walked out looking for the right number.

The door was open. She walked in not knowing what to expect. Karina was on the balcony, wearing a short black dress barely covering her long tanned legs.

"You made it." Karina's smile was seductive, or was it Gabriela's imagination? She handed her a glass of champagne. On any other night, Gabriela would have been taken back by the view from the balcony, this time she couldn't take her eyes of off Karina. She found it hard to swallow and even harder to find the right words.

"Do you greet all strangers like this?" she finally asked.

"What do you mean?"

"I mean, do you let all strangers into your house and greet them with a glass of champagne?" Karina took a sip from her glass, seductively looking right into Gabriela's eyes.

"Nah," she whispered. "Just the cute ones," she answered smiling. Once again Gabriela was speechless. "You are very innocent." Gabriela wasn't sure should she take this as a compliment or an insult.

"Don't judge the book by its cover," she answered bravely. Karina laughed again.

"What if I like the cover?" She replied before she took another sip of champagne.

Without realising Gabriela emptied her drink, anything to calm her nerves and shaky hands. Karina poured them both another glass.

"It's OK," she spoke very softly. "You don't have to be nervous. Imagine we are back in the gallery and there are people around. You were very calm and collected that first night we met. Can I see that Gabriela again?"

"I would like that." Gabriela felt silly and embarrassed for how she came across. Either the cool evening breeze coming from the river or the champagne helped her calm down. And actually enabled them to have a nice, long conversation.

They talked for hours about how they both got there. What they do and what they hope for in the future.

Gabriela came to Ireland from Brazil just over a year ago, and was hoping to make it her home. Karina, daughter of an Iranian women and Spanish man who briefly met in America, spend most of her years in Texas before moving away to travel through Europe. She found her passion for photography and never looked back. She made Dublin her home for most of the year and pit stop while travelling.

Before they knew it, the Sun went down and the night sky fell upon them, it was clear of clouds and full of starts, purple and pink colours bounced of the water in the horizon, nearly as if someone painted it just for them, just for that one night.

"It's getting late." Gabriela looked at her watch. "I should probably go." She didn't want to leave this amazing apartment and go back to her shared room but she didn't want to overstay her welcome either as she wasn't sure of Karina's intentions.

"Are you in a rush?" Karina put down her glass. Gabriela could feel her heart beat once again.

She didn't get a chance to answer before she felt Karina's lips on her lips. So soft, so plump and tasty, it's like something she has never tasted before. Karina unbuttoned the top of her shirt and kissed her neck. Her lips travelled lower with every button she opened.

She kissed Gabriela's breast, her stomach, she slowly started opening her pants, first the button. She looked up at Gabriela with a seductive look on her face, she gave her a wink as she pulled down the zipper and put her hands on Gabriela's hips and pulled her closer while she kissed the bottom of her stomach. Gabriela could feel the rising heat between her legs. She felt paralysed, she never wanted anyone so much.

She couldn't help herself any longer, she reached down and put her hands in Karina's hair. So soft and silky. She pulled Karina up so she could taste her lips again; they kissed slowly, passionately. Her eyes closed, once again it felt as if the time stopped. The whole world stopped just for them, for that moment.

She could feel Karina's hands on her skin, she didn't realise when Karina took off her shirt but she did not complain. She could once again smell her perfume the sweet, musky smell that stayed with her since the night in the gallery. Karina pushed the door open and they slowly moved inside; they didn't stop kissing not for a second.

Gabriela felt a couch behind her, beautiful leather couch, just like the one in the gallery. She sat down and let Karina sit on top of her, with her strong thighs on each side. Gabriela put her hands on Karina's legs, she ran her hands up and down as she felt Karina's hands running up and down her spine. She was kissing her neck, biting her ear.

Gabriela started to taste the beautiful caramel skin she was fantasising about. She wanted to kiss every inch of it, try every corner every hidden secret. She reached under Karina's dress, her body arched with pleasure.

The champagne, the stars and sky outside, the cool breeze, Gabriela shamelessly slipped her finger inside while their bodies perfectly coordinated, danced to the beat of their breath. Slow at first, then a little bit faster as if they have done it so many times before.

Alex

It was already after 9 and Noelle was not yet in the office. Alex went to get her 2nd coffee and she was afraid she will soon run out of excuses to leave her desk. She didn't know what to say or do but for some reason, she just wanted to see her new boss.

Just to get a glimpse of her face and surely all of the feelings that have been awaken in her last week are going to be gone. Just one glimpse to know it was all just an exciting first impression and there is nothing else there. She always had a thing for a powerful, strong, independent woman and she was somewhat excited to be finally working for one, that's probably all it was.

She poured coffee into her cup and went back to her desk, just after deciding to move on with her day, she noticed Noelle's IM changing into green. Is she already in? How did I miss her? She thought to herself as a message popped up on her screen.

Noelle arrived into the office around 9; she parked the car but didn't want to go in just yet. She wasn't ready to face the week. She went to the little café across the street from the office instead and ordered a soya latte with a shot of caramel, she deserved a little treat today. She went upstairs and sat by the window.

She could see the whole street. She loved to just take few minutes out of her day and 'people watch'. Everyone is so busy, so preoccupied with their day and journey to wherever they are rushing. No one notices that it's a lovely sunny morning.

She, however, noticed. She noticed a lot of beauty this weekend. Beauty that was right in front of her eyes but for some reason she was blind to it for so long. She opened her email to make sure she's not missing any meetings but to her delight her dairy for the day was unusually quiet. After the email, she opened her IM, took a deep breath and started typing.

"Hi."

Alex's heart was beating a little faster. "Hi," she replied back within seconds.

"I couldn't wake up this morning. I mean I did but I stayed in bed for a while just thinking." Noelle was always straight forward, she was never afraid to go for what she wanted.

"Well, I can see you're not in the office ☺. All OK?" Alex was keeping the conversation light.

"Stalker." Noelle wasn't sure how to say what she wanted to say next. "Look I sort of knew who you were when I said hi last week."

"Of course you got my email on Friday," Alex responded innocently.

"Not just that," Noelle continued. "I looked into your Instagram and I don't know I really wanted to talk to you."

"That's OK, you want to know who works for you." Alex still kept the conversation light. She was a little confused and a little excited. Was she right all along when she imagined them flirting last week? Was it her imagination or maybe it all actually happened?

"Well, I think it's a little bit more than that. I really wanted to talk to you, get to know you. You sort of fell victim into my trap last week, and I felt bad for not being honest. I'm not sure what it is but you're a very attractive, intriguing woman, Alex."

Alex's head was spinning; her heart felt like it's going to jump out of her chest and she couldn't see anything in front of her eyes, her screen was blurry and she felt like she was going to collapse.

"I didn't expect this," she replied half lying and half relieved as she was trying to convince herself the last two days there was no connection between them.

"Are you free at lunchtime? We could grab something in town or just sit in my car and talk?"

"Is it a question or are you telling me this is what's happening?" Alex was trying to keep her head cool.

"I guess it's happening then." Noelle replied with a smile on her face. Alex couldn't see her but she could imagine it quite clearly.

"I will meet you downstairs at 12:30 then, tell your boss you're taking a long lunch today."

Oh wait, I am your boss, she thought to herself as she closed her PC, took last sip of her coffee and went into the office.

The next few hours were not very productive for either Noelle or Alex. One couldn't believe what she was doing and was wondering where is this going to take her. The other one was not exactly sure what's happening and what to expect from the lunch time get together.

Alex was very charming and quite often found herself an object of desire but she always brushed it off after an innocent flirt. This time however she was not in control as the situation took her by surprise.

"Black Mercedes at the end of the parking lot" said the instructions in the last IM before she left the office. She was walking around the parking looking for the car trying not to look too suspicious. She finally reached her destination with both excitement and confusion inside of her.

She didn't know what to think or expect from this encounter, she was trying not to expect anything more than a quick conversation and both of them laughing the situation off. Alex opened the passenger door.

"Hi," Alex whispered a little uncomfortably, as if she didn't want anyone to hear.

"Hi," said Noelle peaking in from the driver's seat. "Get in." Alex hopped in the passenger seat completely not knowing what to expect. They both smiled at each other, with an innocent teenage like crush look in their eyes.

"So," Noelle was trying to break the silence. "Here we are."

"And where is that?"

"I'm not sure," she laughed nervously. "I did make you protein balls," Noelle pointed at a box of little round protein snacks in the back seat.

"Wow, she's attractive, powerful, she knows what she wants and she cooks". Alex felt a little more comfortable. "Where do I sign up," she made a flirtatious joke which seemed to relax both of them.

"You know," Noelle hesitated. "I have never done this before."

"Done what?" Alex was trying to figure out what are they actually doing.

"This? I mean telling someone I'm thinking of them, I'm into them. I don't know, I'm a married woman. I have a beautiful family and an amazing husband at home." It sounded like she was trying to convince herself.

"And I have a partner at home, yet here we are." Alex smiled, she understood how hard it is to not give into temptation and do what is right rather than what feels right.

"Here we are," Noelle repeated it out loud still questioning what she was doing.

"Don't worry, you haven't done anything wrong. This," Alex took a pause. "This can stay between us, no one has to know and we don't have to talk about this again."

"You think we could do that?" Noelle was a little relieved but more so felt disappointed.

"Yes, I think we can." Alex smiled gently. "We are both adults right?"

"I guess we are." Noelle felt safe, she didn't feel like this with anyone for a long time. She was used to always being in control.

"What if," she looked at Alex again, "what if I don't want that, not talking or acting on my impulses. What if for the first time in my life I want to do something for me. Something that only I know about, something that's separate from my perfect life, marriage, career?"

"I think you need to answer those questions for yourself. I mean if your marriage and life are so perfect what are you doing here?" Alex was trying her best not to lean in and kiss Noelle. She was seduced by her power, looks and now seeing her vulnerable side, she was afraid she can quickly fall for her personality.

She didn't want to do anything she will later regret. She was always a straight shooter and knew she needs to figure out her own relationship before she does anything she can't take back.

"I guess you are right. So we go back to the office and not talk about this again? I don't know what do we do?" Noelle took Alex by the hand, the soft smooth skin she never felt before.

Alex seemed to jump a little she did not anticipate one touch of someone's hand can send shivers through her entire body. This was going to be more difficult than she thought.

"I don't know," Alex replied. "I guess we just need to figure out if this will go away after a while. I mean we can be friends, right?"

"I guess we can." Noelle smiled still holding on to Alex's hand. "It feels so right, its smooth with you, talking and I don't know it's just different."

"I know." Alex smiled and kissed Noelle on the cheek as she opened the door. "Go home and sleep on it, and how about we grab a coffee tomorrow before work?"

"I would really like that." Noelle smiled, she stayed in the car for another while after Alex left. She considered going back to the office but decided to take the rest of the day off. She was hoping seeing her kids and Liam will bring her back to reality and help her forget about this weird attempt at whatever she was trying to accomplish.

Alex came home late that evening, her appetite was gone and she didn't think she will be able to sleep much. She ate the protein balls on the way home smiling to herself. She knew this is going to blow over in a day or two. It's all going to go back to normal.

It always does. She took the dog for a long walk by the sea; she did not sleep much that night yet she was fresh and joyful the next morning.

Gabriela

The rays of morning sunshine came through the window. Gabriela opened her eyes; she was somewhere between reality and imagination. The champagne from last night made her head heavy. She looked at the widely spread curtains and the beautiful view of the river.

Some early morning joggers committed to their morning run were passing by, birds chirping in the background. Karina walked into the room in a white fitted suit. She put on her heels with one hand, holding a cup of freshly brewed coffee with another.

"This is for you," she said to Gabriela while handing her the cup.

"Thank you." Gabriela was still half asleep. "Where are you going on a Sunday morning?" she asked smiling

"Sunday?" Karina seemed amused by the question. "Honey, it's 7 am on a Monday and I am going to work."

"Monday?" Gabriela seemed surprise by the discovery. "Fuck," she shouted as she jumped out of bed. Her tanned body and curly hair looked even darker covered in nothing but a morning sun.

"In a rush?" Karina seemed amused by Gabriela's childlike energy.

"Sort of, yes. I should be at work."

"Why won't you call in sick?" Karina's smile was irresistible; she walked closer to Gabriela and put her hands around her. "Stay in bed, order some breakfast, go down to the pool, relax a little. I should be back shortly after lunch. I just have one meting to take care of."

The idea seemed quite amazing. I mean what would happen if she skipped one day of work. Gabriela looked around. This amazing apartment, view, pool, even coffee smelled so much better, her senses here were somehow elevated. It was either this or her shared room in a small apartment on a busy Dublin Street.

"I guess I could do that this one time." Gabriela pulled Karina closer and gave her a long, passionate kiss.

"Good girl, I will see you soon." Gabriela watched Karina get her keys and phone. She gave her one last smile as she walked out of the apartment. She stayed in bed for a little longer before she indulged in all the treats this place had to offer.

After the trip to the pool and a long steam and sauna sessions, Gabriela entertained herself with Netflix. She didn't realise the clock was approaching 5 and there was still no sign of Karina. Gabriela tried to call her but her phone was off.

Around 6, Gabriela heard two voices outside the apartment before a key turned in the lock and the door opened. Gabriela stood close to the front door wrapped in a towel.

"Oh, this is awkward, for you like," said a blonde girl who entered the apartment.

Karina threw a stern look at the blonde. "Can you wait in the kitchen please, I'll be right there."

"Sure," said the blonde looking Gabriela up and down.

"I am so sorry," said Karina. Gabriela was confused and angry. She ran into the bedroom to put on her clothes.

"Please stop," said Karina. "I am really sorry. I didn't realise you will be here."

"You asked me to stay, remember?" Gabriela was both angry and upset. "To drop everything, skip work and stay and wait for you. What was I thinking."

"I'm sorry, I completely forgot."

"I rang you, your phone was off."

"I know." Karina was trying to calm Gabriela down. "I lost my phone somewhere between leaving here this morning and getting into the office."

"It's OK, enjoy your company. You're obviously busy." Gabriela pointed at the kitchen.

"It's just a friend, also we are not a thing. I get that this doesn't look good but we had one night together, that's all. I don't do 'relationships', kid."

"Point taken." Gabriela put on her top and walked towards the door.

"Look, I'm sorry," Karina put her hands on Gabriela's face and looked into her eyes. "Please look at me, I am really really sorry. My friend popped into the gallery at lunchtime. We grabbed a bite to eat and a glass of wine after. Time sort of got away from me. She just came in for a glass before going home. Please let me make it up to you next weekend?"

It was hard to stay mad at her, Gabriela was once again getting lost in the depths of her eyes, now angry at herself for not being able to walk away from this situation. Karina put her lips on Gabriela's lips. "Pretty please," she whispered.

"I will think about it," Gabriela was trying hard to stay annoyed where all she wanted to do was take Karina in her arms and stay with her, stay for as long as she was able to, as long as she was allowed.

"OK, you think about it," Karina was whispering into Gabriela's ear, moving her cheek against Gabriela's. Her smell was seducing Gabriela all over again.

"I like you, kid," she said as she was walking Gabriela towards the door.

"I normally don't do second dates," she added as she closed the door.

Gabriela was annoyed with that comment but couldn't help to feel somehow special. A car was waiting outside to take her back to her shared bedroom in her apartment where she went straight to bed. She closed her eyes and replayed the whole weekend in her mind over and over and over again.

Noelle and Alex

The morning came rather quickly, and even though Alex didn't sleep a wink, she felt refreshed and joyous. She hopped out of bed early, took a shower, picked one of her best clothes, a nice fitted black slacks and a tight white shirt. She got out of the house early and headed straight for the coffee shop.

To her surprise, Noelle was already there. She was at the counter in a tight black dress and matching 6 inch heels. Her blond hair flawlessly resting on her shoulders.

"Good Morning," said Noelle with a big smile on her face.

"Good Morning," Alex replied with an even bigger smile.

"What are you having?"

"Americano please, with some coconut milk," said Alex looking at the cashier. A nice Brazilian girl was smiling at them from behind the counter. Alex realised she never noticed her before.

"Soya latte please, we will have it here." Noelle flirtatiously looked Alex up and down. "You look nice."

"Thank you," Alex got a little red. "So do you, I mean you look stunning in your Tuesday attire." Noelle laughed out loud.

"Cute and cheeky; now I'm in trouble."

"One Soya Latte, one black with coconut milk," called out the smiley girl form behind the counter.

"Thank you, Gabriela," said Alex reading the name tag as she took both cups.

"Should we go upstairs? It's quiet there at this time, we will be able to talk," said Noelle pointing at a little door at the side of the café.

"Upstairs?" Alex seemed surprised. "I didn't know they had upstairs."

"Oh I'm sure there is a lot of things you don't know." Noelle was still flirtatious, as much as Alex enjoyed it, she was also a little afraid. Afraid of not being able to control herself if there is no one around them.

"Lead the way," she replied. Despite carrying two hot mugs, she still managed to open the door and let Noelle ahead. It clearly impressed Noelle.

As they walked up the round stairs, she wanted to stop, just for a second to push Alex against the wall and lean against her body. She wanted to kiss her; she wondered what her lips would feel like, would they be soft, what do they taste like. She stopped herself, considering Alex was carrying two cups of hot beverage she didn't want to scold her or put an end to this romance before it even started.

Upstairs was indeed empty; just one guy eating his breakfast muffin and drinking his super-sized coffee in the corner. Dressed very sharply in a suit and tie, reading eagerly through his notes. They picked a table on the other side of the room, as far as possible to get some privacy. They sat next to each other on a brown leather sofa.

"This is nice," said Alex to break the silence. "And thank you for the coffee," she continued as she raised her mug.

"Cheers." Noelle also raised her latte. "No problem and I think we should do this every day, you know just to start your day on a positive note."

"Sure," said Alex, "very positive." She smiled that innocent, cute smile. Noelle once again wanted to lean in but once again she stopped herself.

"How was your evening?" Alex asked.

"It was good, I was thinking about you," Noelle was playfully running her hand through her blond strands.

"I thought we were not supposed to do that," Alex was feeling relaxed and playful. "You know think about each other."

"Is that so," Noelle laughed out loud. "How was yours?"

"Well, I didn't eat, I didn't sleep much and I was thinking about you too. I wanted to text you but I didn't think it was OK."

"No, I don't think it is." Noelle seemed upset. "But I want you to. Do you have Pinterest?"

"No, I don't, why anything good on it?"

"Well, I could pin some things and maybe you can pin some things too and that way we will know we are thinking of each other."

"I like that." Alex enjoyed this game, it was innocent and spontaneous, different to what her life has been over the past while. She liked spending time with Noelle it was easy and fun.

"There is my log in." Noelle handed Alex a piece of paper. "Get an account log in and follow me, that way I can see what you're up to."

"Oh, you will spy on me now?" Alex laughed. "Are you not doing that already?"

"It was once OK, I looked at your Insta once." Noelle was now the one with rosy cheeks, she felt ashamed but also happy to have taken such outrageous steps.

"This is nice, you know," she put her hand on Alex's leg. "Oh I'm sorry," she took it away as soon as she realised what she has done.

"It's ok," Alex put her hand on Noelle's hand and gave it a little squeeze. She felt the same feeling like the day before, like electricity going through her body. She didn't take her hand away. "I know this is a little confusing," she smiled gently, "for both of us."

"I have never done anything like this, never felt such a pull towards anyone."

"And it will probably go away soon." Alex was in similar situations before, but it always went away after few weeks of innocent fantasies that didn't go anywhere. The reality always took back its place. She never acted on anything and didn't think she will act on anything this time.

"We can't deny the pull, or whatever you want to call it," she smiled as she moved her hand and touched Noelle's cheek. Noelle closed her eyes and leaned into Alex's hand. She gave it a little kiss thinking that will have to be enough, for now.

"So what do we do?" Noelle was looking for some guidance, she felt like Alex knows what to do and how not let anything happen.

"We wait," Alex laughed at her own words. "We wait till it goes and you don't feel it anymore."

"What if it won't go away?"

"It will, trust me." Alex smiled, she took a sip of her coffee. "I wonder how many coconuts they had to milk to sort out my coffee?" They both laughed.

"It's going to be OK, nothing will happen. Just take it easy on yourself and don't feel guilty," the warmth in Alex's voice was comforting.

"I guess you're right." Noelle felt safe in her company, even though she didn't know her that long. She leaned towards Alex and gave her a big hug.

"I'm going on holidays after this week. I'm sure it will all go away by the time I'm back. Thank you for not making a big deal out of me trying to chat you up."

"Well, I did think I had a *Fatal Attraction* kind of scenario on my hands so I'm glad to see it's not that." They both laughed again. "I was even getting my CV ready in case things go bad."

"Please don't," Noelle looked concerned. "Regardless of what happens or doesn't happen, please don't ever feel you need to do that. We can always sort something out, something that suits you. If you feel uncomfortable because of my, well rather unprofessional behaviour, we can think of a different office or whatever suits you."

"You were not unprofessional," Alex smiled. She knew Noelle is obviously feeling bad for what happened. "Look nothing happened here OK, we clicked, connected, might be for many reasons. I'm a new face and you know us eastern-Europeans, we are sort of exotic to you pasty blond Irish, it's all good."

"I would say you're exotic to everyone." Noelle felt much calmer once again she took comfort from Alex, comfort she didn't really know before. She felt like she can breathe and be herself for the first time in her life. "Also we don't know what sort of scenario we have on our hands just yet do we?"

She was the one being cheeky now. Alex enjoyed her wit and courage to say whatever she felt like.

They finished their coffee and went into the office to get on with their days. They spend lunch together every day and met for coffee in the morning before work. Friday came quickly and they were both a little sad to finish their week long romance.

They didn't act on anything and just enjoyed getting to know each other. Laughing, telling each other stories, getting to know more and more about each other's life's and developing some sort of connection neither of them knew before. But now it was all about to end and after two weeks apart they were sure what they will have is a friendship. They exchanged couple of emails that day and decided it's better not to see each other before they finish work.

Alex looked at her mailbox just before she left work on Friday afternoon and found this.

"Thank you, for this amazing week, Alex. What a whirlwind it has been. I really don't know what to think and what I'm feeling but I know for sure that you have my back and I have yours, and you will always have a friend in me. Now go on and enjoy your two weeks of peace, just don't make anyone else crazy around here when I'm gone.

Now seriously, thank you for your kindness and understanding, whatever happened in my head I wasn't sure of you seemed to know how to maintain and navigate this pick and mix of emotion and desire, and for that I will always be grateful. You sort of saved me from myself.

Your dear friend,

Noelle"

Alex read those words with a mixed feeling of happiness and disappointment. She knew she didn't want this to end at the same time it was too dangerous to keep going. Not like this. She made up her mind this week. She knew she wanted this more than she was willing to admit, and if she doesn't pursue it she will regret this for the rest of her life.

Even thought she had 2 weeks to cool off and go back to her reality, she didn't want to. Not this time. Both the burning desire and curiosity as to what this might be were taking over her body and mind. She felt as if some out of this world power was consuming her, like a wild fire and this time she couldn't fight it, she didn't want to fight it. She wanted to surrender to it fully, with all that she had.

She went home that evening and waited till Niamh came back. When Niamh walked in the door, as hard as it was she got all her courage and bravery to do what she though was right for everyone. She was tired of fighting, tired of pretending, tired of trying to fix herself, fix something that was not broken. It just didn't fit in Niamh's world, and she knew if she wants something, someone so much what she has here was over.

"Oh you're home," Niamh said as she walked into the room and put on the light. "Why are you sitting in the dark?"

"Niamh, please sit down. We have to talk." Alex replied, holding on to the courage born out of nowhere. She knew she has made up her mind and needs to do what she felt was right. What was right for her.

Gabriela

"Do these two look overly friendly to you?" Gabriela pointed at two women waiting for their coffee. She saw them around before but not together. They were both well dressed, they looked like they made more effort than usual. She observed them discreetly while serving other customers.

"Who?" Her colleague asked. Gabriela pointed to the right.

"Oh," she seemed a little disappointed. "I don't think so. I think they are just good friends."

"I don't know, they look like something more."

"Gabriela," said her colleague with slight irritation, "Life is not an episode of the L Word you know, people don't just hook up on every corner."

"I guess you're right," a slight smile showed up on Gabriela's face. You have no idea, she thought to herself.

The answer to Gabriela's question if the friendly couple was something more than friendly will have to wait a little longer. Even though the two women came here every morning, she didn't notice anything that would satisfy her suspicion. Gabriela liked looking at people, observing. Her favourite thing was to grab a coffee at lunch time and go sit on a bench in town and just watch life go by.

Back in Brazil, she was a therapist, for now however, she was only able to work on a student visa while she practiced English, not that it needed any practicing. She often wondered how would her life look like if she was born in America or Europe; being able to travel and work without a visa and actually do what she was passionate about. Friday night came quicker than usual. Gabriela got home and just as she made peace with not hearing from Karina all week, her phone lit up.

"Hey, You, I know I wasn't around last two weeks. Do you fancy another adventure?"

Gabriela's friend fell silent after she met her prince charming that night in the gallery. God only knows what she has in store this time. With weekend around the corner and no plans, Gabriela felt a little curious.

"What have you in mind?" she replied

"I have tickets for another art exhibition, this one is a little less high class it's for some student thing, want to come?"

Oh no, was the first thought on Gabriela's mind, on the other hand maybe it's a chance to see her own princess charming again.

"Sure," she replied without hesitation.

"Great, collect you in an hour."

Gabriela made a lot of effort again to look like the best version of herself. It made her laugh when she looked in the mirror as it reminded her of the two ladies in the coffee shop. She still wondered if there was something going on between them; she wanted to know as she could feel the romance in the air and her gut feeling never let her down.

Tonight, however, she was hopefully going to see Karina again. She must be around galleries all the time, what else do people like her do? This conclusion seemed very logical. I could just call her, the thought came to her mind couple of times over the week. She, however, talked herself out of it each time, that would seem too desperate and one thing Gabriela didn't want was to look desperate.

The taxi arrived; her friend was as eager to get to the gallery as she was the first time around. This time Gabriela shared her enthusiasm. When they arrived to the location, however the level of excitement dropped. No windows or sign above large doors, no fancy dressed guy to open the door for them, no well-dressed and spoken people and no sing of 'art'.

They stood for a while wondering if they got to the right place, google maps pointed to the door behind them. That couldn't be it. It looked more like an abandoned basement than cave of wonders.

"Should we knock and see?" Bruna's enthusiasm might have dropped but not her determination.

"And this is how we die," said Gabriela before agreeing to go in.

The door opened and a young man asked the girls for their jackets, after a little hesitation, they both decided to hold on to their belongings. The stairs leading down seemed to go on forever and with each step the smell of dampness grew stronger.

"Seriously, what are we doing here again?"

"I am not entirely sure, someone told me this was an exhibition?"

They finally reached the bottom of the stairs. They walked into a room where a big projector cast a movie on a wall. A home-made, student short movie. The same movie seemed to be playing over and over.

Another room had a couple of pictures in cheap frames hanging from a rope and then another had a sculpture made from toilet rolls.

"What is this again?" Gabriela asked as she looked at the tickets for the first time.

"1st year Student Art Exhibition," she read it out loud. "Bruna, what the fuck?" She could no longer hide her disappointment.

"OK, I dropped the ball on this one. You want to grab a drink considering we are already out?" Bruna asked with her big puppy like eyes and innocent smile.

"As long as we can get out of here I will even go for a drink, anything is better than this."

As they moved back towards the stairs, they left the damp smell and dust eagerly behind them. With each step, they could grasp more and more of the fresh air sneaking in from behind a big steel door. They both seemed relieved once the door was closed behind them.

"Never and I mean ever again," Gabriela was trying to make sense of this experience.

"Did you not like the toilet paper thing? It will come in handy after they drink all that cheap wine." Both girls were now laughing out loud as they walked towards a bar.

A nice little bar was located just around the corner. They ordered some drinks and sat by the window.

"So?" Gabriela was interested in her friends intentions. "Why did we go there again?"

"I really don't know," Bruna replied. "I really thought this was legit."

"And why do you always seem so eager to go to those places anyway?"

"Galleries?" Bruna asked, Gabriela shook her head in reply. "Well, it started in college, you know the guys in there would always be a little older, a little more sophisticated. Not like the ones I knew."

"And you just keep going because?" Gabriela's curiosity was not yet satisfied.

"Because one day, I will meet my future husband in one of those galleries, he will be in town for a weekend, on a business trip and he will notice me. He will come towards me, slowly and he will ask me what my name is and we will talk, for hours, but it will feel like minutes. And there will be people, everywhere but he will only have eyes for me.

"He will bring me wine and at the end of the night he will leave me his card. His car will drop me back home. We will say goodbye with a gentle kiss. I will call him after a few days, he will come to town again, just to see me.

"We will have dinner, he will take me to his hotel to show me the view from his room. We will make sweet love all night and..." Bruna looked at Gabriela's confused but highly amused face. "Well, you know how it goes," she rushed to finish the fantasy.

"And they lived happily ever after," Gabriela finished for her. "Yes, I know how it goes."

"Do you have an awful step mother and step sisters in this story or do you sleep for a 100 years?" She felt like this needed a slight dash of mockery.

"You can mock all you want," said Bruna. "Not everyone is cold hearted or gave up on love, you know. I still want romance, flowers, long conversations by the fire."

"And a rich husband?" Gabriela could not help herself.

"That would also be nice, yes." Bruna was now laughing.

They finished their drink and headed for the door. As they approached the taxi, Bruna looked at Gabriela.

"Hold on, you never told me why did you come here?"

"Well," said Gabriela as she got into the taxi. "You see, I had my long conversation by the candle light, the time did indeed stop, then we had dinner and she showed me all her views. I was just hoping to see her again." As the door closed and taxi pulled away, Bruna was left on the street with a look of both shock and amusement on her face.

Gabriela arrived at her destination 20 minutes later. She stood on the opposite side of the street looking up at the balcony. The light in the room was on but she could not see any movement. Is she there? She wondered.

What am I even going to say? What am I going to tell her? Gabriela grew more nervous with each minute passing by.

"This is madness," she said out loud just as she heard a familiar voice behind her.

"I wondered if I will ever see you again. I didn't think you will be stalking me though," Karina appeared out of nowhere in a tight black jogging outfit.

"I…" Gabriela froze. "I am so sorry, this is not what it looks like."

"What is it then?" Karina continued playfully. Her hair was up in a pony tail it complemented her cheek bones and a beautiful face.

"OK it sort of is," Gabriela smiled. "But not really I mean."

"Do you want to come up?" Karina took Gabriela's hand and moved towards the apartment.

"Yes," Gabriela whispered as they crossed the street. "Very much so."

Noelle

Time seemed to fly since Noelle left work on Friday, between travelling and trying to get everyone settled into their rooms in a little villa in a south of France. Noelle opened her eyes; to her surprise it was already 10. She normally liked to get up early even during days off or holidays.

She liked to go for a little walk and sip her coffee outside on the veranda before anyone else was up. It was her quiet time, her happy place. Today, however, she didn't want to face the day. She loved family holidays, especially on such an occasion as 15 year wedding anniversary.

This time around she couldn't wait for it to pass so she can go back home, so she can go back to work and see Alex. During last minute change of plans, Noelle invited Liam's parents to tag along. More help with the boys, and more distractions for Liam; she felt guilty but also relieved. She could hear voices coming from downstairs.

The boys laughter always brought a smile to her face; there is nothing quite like a child's laugh. She got up to look outside the window. The sun was peaking from behind a little hill up ahead, the trees still had their beautiful leaves rustling in the wind. It was a picture perfect holiday, like everything in her life.

She closed her eyes and imagined Alex's hair, the beautiful brown hair matching colours with her eyes, and those dimples only visible when she smiles. Noelle closed the window and went back to bed, still keeping her eyes closed she imagined how would it feel to have Alex's arms around her. How would it feel to put her face in Alex's hair, to get lost in her scent. To feel her skin.

As she fell deeper and deeper into her fantasy, she felt warmth between her legs. She bit her lip, her hand travelled down her body . She put her hand between her legs imagining it was Alex. She opened her eyes worrying that someone might open the door any minute. With a faint smile on her face, she reached for her phone.

Now Miss Alex, let's give you something to think about, she thought to herself as she opened Pinterest. I always liked cycling, she said with a cheeky smile as she pinned some female cyclist in tight outfits. She went on to the videos and picked Ariana Grande's *Side to side* to keep with the theme.

Now something sweet, she thought as she went through pages and pages of pins before she finally picked the perfect one.

"No matter how far away we are from each other in distance, or in time, when we look up into the clear night sky, we will always see the same moon."

Noelle took few more minutes before she put her phone down and went to the bathroom to take a cold shower. She thought maybe that will help and bring her back to reality. To her picture perfect reality.

Alex

Alex got up early this Monday morning after spending the last few nights in the spare room. Most of her clothes were now packed and ready for a move. She seemed to be having the same conversation with Niamh over and over again for the last few days, every time without really being able to explain what has changed.

She changed and she knew she is no longer able to stay in this relationship. She tried, she did everything she could over the years, she jumped through every hurdle, she worked on herself and finally she realised she was not the problem. She loved Niamh and she wished her all the best she knew whoever their paths need to part.

The conversation seemed to go the same way, first anger, some shouting, then Niamh would calm down. She seemed to be understanding Alex's reasoning and was agreeing with it, and then anger again. It was exhausting, it was hard and it seemed to go in circles.

Just like all their fights and all the last chances she has given Alex over the years. A little ironic, Alex thought to herself. Niamh was the one who constantly gave her all the ultimatums, yet it was Alex who at the end realised they are just not compatible.

Alex put most of her clothes in the car, she was going to stay in a hotel for a few days till she can find an apartment. She knew staying in their place is neither good or healthy. They both need space and time to heal.

As she drove through town, she thought long and hard about the decision she made. She felt with every fibre in her body it was the right one. For some reason, she also knew she wants to pursue Noelle, even though it might go either way she wanted to try, to give herself a chance.

After spending a couple of days in her company, she felt herself falling for her new boss and she couldn't ignore her feelings. The desire was so strong it felt as if a burning petrol was running through her veins. Alex arrived at work just before 10, she parked the car and looked at her phone.

She opened Pinterest with a slight glim of hope. Surely she won't even be online, she's in some beautiful location with her husband and family, the chances of her even thinking of me are slim. Despite the negative thoughts, she still started following Noelle's profile. Alex smiled, the pins were quite intriguing. The tight lycra clothes and cycling shorts on the super fit models body.

"I'm sure that's how they would look on you," Alex said out loud, she looked around to make sure she is alone. The choice of song is really interesting. She laughed. She also noticed the pin in the recent folder. Left there for everyone to see only 30 minutes ago.

It might be there for everyone to see, but it was only for her to understand. And understand she did. Alex closed her eyes, she replayed their conversations, especially their first chat in the car. Just a week ago, they both sat in the car on this very parking spot.

They sat, they talked, they innocently looked into each other's eyes and then their hands met, the electricity, the fire it all started in that moment. One touch has changed so much in both of their lives. Alex wasn't sure how is this going to go and what is going to happen.

She doubted there will be a happy ending to this story but she knew she wants this more than anything in her life. She wanted to try, she knew the risks and she was willing to take them. The car door opened and Alex slowly walked to the office.

It's going to be a long two weeks, she thought as she walked into the elevator.

Gabriela

The apartment was spacious and sophisticated, just as Gabriela remembered. Fresh flowers and candles all over the living room and the bedroom set a nice, relaxing mood. She noticed Karina had her pictures all over the hall, she didn't see them the last time, she was too preoccupied.

The one thing she remembered so well was the view from the balcony. She took out 2 glasses and opened a bottle of prosecco while Karina was in the shower. She went to the balcony and enjoyed the view, the peace, the moon light bouncing of the water and the gentle wind playing in the background.

She felt silly, even intrusive being caught like that standing on the street looking up at the windows, trying to find a courage to call. She didn't recognise herself or her behaviour. Normally cool headed, she felt as if she was losing her mind thinking about Karina and the weekend they spend in this very place. On the other hand, she felt like it was right, like she was supposed to come here this Friday evening, just to see what happens.

Either way she was here now. Gabriela heard music coming from inside, smooth jazz from what she was able to hear. She looked into the apartment and saw Karina in a black, light bath robe with water still dripping down her legs and arms; the drops looked like little diamonds glowing on her caramel skin.

"Would you like some food?" Karina asked as if nothing happened, as if this evening was planned and she didn't just caught Gabriela stalking her.

"Sure," said Gabriela, she wasn't sure what's this game they are playing but she was happy to participate.

"Thai OK?" Karina asked without waiting for response as she started making the order. Gabriela smiled, she wasn't sure if she liked that but she was playing along. She was an intruded in this perfect evening and she was just happy to be here. To be in Karina's presence.

"Food will be here in 30 minutes." Karina broke the silence as she reached for her glass. "So, you can tell me now what were you doing downstairs," she continued.

"I'm really sorry." That's all Gabriela was able to get out. "I don't normally do that. I don't know, I just went out with a friend and got here afterwards." She took a pause and took a sip of her drink. "Truth be told, I was looking for the courage to call you."

"And would you have called me?" Karina asked with a smile on her face.

"I don't know," Gabriela started to feel a little bit more comfortable.

"Well, good thing I went out for a run then."

"Why didn't you call me?" Gabriela asked. "After that weekend."

"I didn't have your number, remember I told you I lost my phone and I figured you will at least text me. But you didn't, did you?"

"That makes sense." Gabriela felt silly and childish. Instead of wondering all this time she should have just send a text.

"It's OK, you are here now," said Karina as she walked towards Gabriela. She put her glass down on the kitchen island and put her hands around her face. "Your eyes are beautiful," she said as she kissed Gabriela, that long, passionate, sweet kiss that send shivers all over her body.

They never talked about the unfortunate circumstances in which they met that evening, as if it didn't matter. What mattered is the connection, the desire and the passion they felt for each other in this moment in time. Gabriela did, however, tell a story of how her evening unravelled. The desperate visit to what she thought is going to be another gallery.

It made Karina laugh and appreciate her perseverance, even though all it would take is a text. The evening went smooth, they laughed and talked and drank champagne. They sat on the balcony enjoying each other's company and the view of the river covered in moon light.

Alex

This week was going extremely slow. Alex went to the café each morning to grab her morning dose of Italian brew. She sat by the window staring up at the sky, trying to make sense of what is happening. She didn't know if the brief not even affair she had with Noelle is going to evaporate over the two weeks she was away. Away with her family and her husband.

The pins came and went but what are the wordless pins worth, they couldn't talk, they couldn't communicate. She didn't know what Noelle is thinking or feeling; does she miss her, how could she they literally just met. The thoughts were driving her crazy. She tried to distract herself with work but didn't feel very productive.

It was a sunny Thursday afternoon and Alex was ready to go out for her lunchtime walk around town. She threw last glance at her screen and noticed flashing IM in the corner. She thought she was imagining it, she sat down to take a better look. When she opened the message her heart nearly jumped out of her chest.

"Hey," typed Noelle. "I'm not sure if your still here but I just wanted to say I am thinking of you."

"Hey," Alex replied quickly. "I am thinking of you too."

"There is not a second in my day where I am not thinking about you," Noelle continued. "This is crazy I know. But being away from you it doesn't feel right." Alex had a huge smile on her face and her heart was still pounding.

"I'm so happy to hear from you." Alex was trying to keep the conversation light.

"I couldn't not reach out to you. I needed you to know you're on my mind all the time. I feel bad I'm here in this beautiful place, my kids are running around playing and laughing and I just want to put my headphones on and think about you. What it would be like, feel like to…" she didn't continue the sentence.

Maybe she run out of courage, Alex thought.

"It's OK, you will be back soon we can talk."

"I don't want to talk." Noelle paused once again. "I'm sorry I have to go. I will try and ping you before the week is over."

"OK." Alex was both excited by the message and sad that she couldn't see her. What she would give to be with Noelle right now. To touch her face, taste her lips.

"Hey," the message continued. "I am afraid that I will break your heart as I don't know what I want." Alex smiled at the screen.

"Just don't break your own heart, I'm a big girl, I can handle myself." Noelle smiled on the other side of the screen.

"OK, gorgeous, go and chat soon."

The green light turned black before Alex had a chance to reply.

Alex took a couple of minutes to compose herself and collect her thoughts before she was able to move on with her day.

"Hey," she heard a voice coming from behind. "A couple of us are going to the food market to grab some lunch, want to join?"

"Sure," Alex replied enthusiastically. She thought it would be better not to be alone right now. A distraction seemed like what she needed to save her from her own thoughts.

It was a beautiful day and having the office in town gave so many possibilities. Alex and a couple of colleagues walked to the nearby park where a fresh food stalls appeared every week. It was nice to just talk to people, get to know them and leave the contemplations of life and relationships behind her. Even if it was just for an hour.

Gabriela

The morning Sun sneaked in through the blinds casting its mighty spell over the room, the warmth of it on Gabriela's back woke her up. She lifted her head and wiped the sleep from her eyes when she noticed Karina sitting on the balcony with her coffee in one hand and a book in the other. She sat down on the edge of the bed and took this moment in.

Karina looked like one of her pictures, pure, beautiful and somewhat majestic. Gabriela stayed silent as she didn't want to ruin this perfect moment, she wanted it to last forever, she wanted the world to stop. She looked at Karina's almond shaped eyes, her caramel skin shimmering in the morning sun like the water in the river.

She was at peace, she felt home. If a person can be a home this was it. A sound of a ferry in the distance broke the perfect silence.

"It's beautiful, isn't it," said Karina as she looked into the room from her seat.

"It is."

"Come over here," Karina continued playfully. Gabriela wrapped her body in a soft white sheet and came out to the balcony, the breeze moved her curly waves up and down. She bend down to give Karina a morning kiss and sat down next to her.

They stayed in silence and enjoyed looking at the birds playfully flying in the distance, chirping loudly as they moved up and down in perfect harmony. Gabriela closed her eyes and took in a deep breath of the cool breeze while the sun was warming up her skin.

"You can stay for a while." Karina made what sounded like an offer. "That is if you don't have plans."

"I don't." Gabriela was happy to be a part of this for as long as she could. She didn't care about the apartment or the view or the champagne in the evening. She cared about Karina, she felt good in her company.

"What would you like to do?" Gabriela asked. Karina put out her hand and as soon as Gabriela took it in hers, she pulled her on to her lap. She started to unwrap the sheets from around her body.

"I can tell you who I would like to do." Karina was playful and seductive. "You have a beautiful body, you shouldn't cover it." Gabriela's now naked nipples became hard from the breeze.

Karina looked her in the eye as she put her lips around them. She started to run her tongue down Gabriela's body, her chest, her stomach, she lowered herself down.

"Can anyone see us?" Gabriela whispered.

"No," smiled Karina. "Trust me, no one can see us here." It seemed like Gabriela didn't care anyway. All she could do is to give over to this pleasure. She was the tool in Karina's hands and she let her do whatever she felt like.

Karina lowered herself down as she continued kissing Gabriela's brown skin. Leaving a trail of goosebumps along the way. She slipped her tongue between her legs, Gabriela pushed herself forward and put her hand on Karina's head. Her back arched with pleasure.

She closed her eyes and let herself be lost in the moment. Time stopped just as she wanted and she could no longer feel the cool breeze. The heat of the sun and her body was a dominant feeling. She moaned with pleasure and as Karina pulled herself back up she leaned against her body.

They stayed like this for a while. Wrapped in nothing but the sun and each other's arms. Karina now gently run her hand against Gabriela's skin, up and down her spine. It was like heaven, or rather hell on earth as Gabriela knew this is going to end soon. And the longing for this will leave her day dreaming for days.

Alex

"I didn't think I will see you again," Michelle broke the silence. "I'm glad you are here."

"I know, I went quiet for a little while," Alex smiled. "I made some decisions and I guess I was sort of busy sorting things out. I don't think I need to come here anymore I just wanted this last session, for closure."

"So, what would you like to talk about today," Michelle asked with a smile on her face.

"I don't know really, I'm happy you know." Alex took a pause to collect her thoughts. "I mean I did just take all my stuff and moved into a hotel till I can find something but I'm at peace. There is no fighting, no arguments, no trying to work on myself or fixing myself."

"You do look at ease," Michelle was glad to see the progress in her new client.

"Thank you," said Alex. "I know it only has been few sessions but all your questions and exercise, it really helped me."

"It doesn't matter how many sessions you do, you were ready." Michelle put her pen and notebook on the table, as if she didn't need it anymore. Alex didn't need it. "So what is the plan now, what do you want to do?"

"I want to live, be free to do what I want, feel love and passion again." Alex smiled a big hopeful smile.

"That sounds great and that person you met, is she the reason?"

"Not really." Alex shifted in her chair. "I mean in some ways yes, she helped me realise that I want more from life. I am not ready to settle for something that how can I phrase it doesn't spark joy. I want to feel passion and love and acceptance and gratitude."

"And you feel those things now."

"Yes," replied Alex. "I do, I feel them from the moment I wake up to the moment I go to sleep. Don't get me wrong it was really hard, to make this decision, I think it took me 3 years if not more. But when I finally did, a huge weight was lifted and I was able to breathe again.

"It's funny how you don't realise how bad something is until you are out of the situation. This is good for both of us. Niamh deserves to be happy and we were just too different, I think."

"Just take your time to heal," said Michelle. "Don't rush into anything just take some time to get to know yourself again. Enjoy you." Michelle smiled. "I'm glad to hear you are doing well, you do look and seem much happier than you were few weeks ago when you walked through that door."

"Yes, I was quite miserable," Alex nodded. "It feels like it wasn't me you know like I was in a sort of a haze, just waking up getting on with my day, getting on with life. It's not who I am anymore".

"No," Michele agreed. "You are hungry for life, for the next adventure that awaits you."

"I am, you know I was told I have too high of an expectations of life, that life is not a fairy tale or I don't know. I refuse to believe that, I want to believe that life is amazing."

"It can be," Michelle smiled looking at the clock. "Life can be whatever you want it to be."

They had another 15 minutes left but Alex was happy to leave it there. She wanted to say bye to her new therapist and thank her for the work they had done. She was happy, free of any boundaries especially the ones in her head, the boundaries which were not even hers.

Alex walked out of the building and bought a coffee from a nearby café. It was a lovely Saturday morning, the sky was blue and the sun was spreading its shine across the surface of the sea. She sat down on the bench and took out her phone, a notification came on Pinterest. The message was of course from Noelle.

"Good Morning. gorgeous, I just wanted to say hi and wish you a lovely weekend. I miss you and I can't wait to see you."

"Hey," Alex typed quickly hoping she can catch Noelle. "Good morning to you too, I hope you are having a nice time away."

"I am," Noelle was typing. "I mean I wish you could be here with me. There is so much I would like to show you, so many places I would like to take you to."

"Maybe someday," Alex replied still not knowing what Noelle's intentions were.

"Hopefully someday," a reply came quickly. "Right, I'm losing WIFI here and I have to get ready for lunch. Just wanted to say I'm thinking of you."

"I am thinking of you too," Alex replied before she put her phone in her pocket.

She sat on the bench overlooking the sea, she wanted to stay in this peaceful moment half present half in a day dream. She imagined the moment Noelle comes back to the office. She won't be able to do what she wants, not with all the people around. She didn't know what Noelle wants from this brief relationship.

All the promises sounded great in her head, at the same time she knew Noelle is married with kids, you don't just walk away from that. Not for someone you just met. Alex didn't care how this is going to end, even a hope of a brief experience was enough for her to take the chance, to take the risk and be all in. That's the only way she knew how to do things, she couldn't do anything being only one foot in the door.

She had to open the door fully and explore the possibilities, no matter the end result. Life is too short to hesitate and live only half awake, she did that for so long, now her life deserved living 100% at the time.

Noelle

The plane landed ahead of schedule. Noelle couldn't believe in what she was doing. She was not supposed to be back in the office for another week nor was she supposed to be back from her holidays for another 4 days. It was a sunny Wednesday morning in Dublin and the sky was unusually blue, not one cloud was visible on the horizon.

August brought a beautiful late summer, she thought as she stepped out on the hot tarmac. She rushed through passport control and to bag collection. She left her family in France and told Liam she needed to be back in the office. This was not an unusual occurrence.

Owning your own business is demanding, they could live the life they did because of her work so Liam never gave her a hard time. She felt bad for leaving the boys but they were having a blast with their grandparents. They loved their company and wouldn't even notice she was missing for the last few days of their holiday, that thought made her feel better.

Their anniversary dinner was planned for tonight, that made her feel both sad and guilty however, she couldn't be herself, or make herself enjoy the moment with what she was feeling. The unknown feeling took over her whole existence, her body mind and spirit were all craving the same thing. She couldn't wait to come back and look at Alex's face. This whole situation made her feel crazy but she couldn't hold back any longer.

The taxi pulled outside the house. Noelle dropped her bag and took a quick shower. She threw on a white blouse and black skirt and put on a pair of 6 inch heels Oh I missed you, she thought as she slipped them on her feet. She looked in the mirror to put on make-up and fix her hair. This will have to do, she thought as she left the house.

Her black Mercedes pulled in the parking lot 20 minutes later. The traffic wasn't too bad at this time of the day, she missed the lunch time rush. She opened her laptop and connected it to the WIFI. She was happy to see Alex's IM on green,

"Hey," she started typing…

Alex

Alex looked at her phone in hope she will hear from Noelle. The last time they briefly talked was on Monday morning. She saw a new pin from this morning, two actually one said:

'Good Morning, Sunshine' and had a picture of coffee in the background. Alex was sure this was meant for her. It brought a smile on her face but didn't compare to the real thing. The second pin was a little bit more serious.

'In the end, we only regret the chances we didn't take, the relationships we were afraid to have and the decisions we waited too long to make'.

Alex wasn't sure what that meant, she was trying not to read too much into this or make something grow in her head. It's just words, all of this just words and pretty pictures. She knew Noelle will be back in a week and they will be able to talk. She scrolled through some pins and picked one for Noelle. She will see it whenever she comes back here, Alex thought.

'If you don't go after what you want, you will never have it'.

She knew she was a bit cheeky but she didn't want to play games, she knew what she wanted and hoped Noelle has the same idea. Alex looked at her PC it was already after lunch, she was so preoccupied with work she didn't even notice the time passing by. An IM showed up on the right hand corner of her screen just as she was getting up to grab a late lunch.

"Hey."

"Well, hello, stranger," Alex replied.

"I'm in the parking lot, come down." Alex's heart stopped, she couldn't believe what she was reading.

"Stop messing with my head," she replied in disbelief.

"Come down and look for yourself. Same spot." Noelle's status turned into offline.

Alex was trying to catch a breath; her heart was beating so fast she thought it will jump out of her chest. She felt light headed. She didn't understand how just a thought of seeing someone can make you feel intoxicated. The elevator seemed to be taking ages to come.

She finally got in, the silence enhanced the sound of her own heart, beating like mad. The door opened, she walked to the end of the parking lot, at the very corner, she saw a black Mercedes indeed parked in its usual spot.

Alex and Noelle

Noelle was sitting in the car impatiently looking at the elevator door every time it opened. She still couldn't believe what she was doing and she didn't have a clue what exactly her plan was. It was not like her not to have one; she was always the dominant one in every relationship, during every meeting this time she knew she will go soft as soon as Alex gets in the car; she knew and she couldn't do anything about it, anything other than surrender…possibly for the first time in her life . She finally saw Alex coming out of the corner after what felt like eternity.

She was wearing a navy suit and a light blue shirt, her long brown hair bouncing flawlessly as she walked towards the car. The door opened and the big brown eyes and dimples appeared in front of her.

"Hey," Alex said casually.

"Get in," Noelle rushed her.

"What are you doing here?" Alex asked with a big smile on her face.

"I couldn't stay away, I guess," Noelle answered.

"But your holidays?"

"I came home early. I started forgetting your face when I closed my eyes and it was upsetting me."

"You could have looked at my picture." Alex's attempt at releasing tension with humour worked as it indeed made Noelle laugh.

"I couldn't kiss a picture, now could I?" Noelle said boldly. Alex looked her up and down she was wearing a tight white blouse. The buttons were open a little bit too low; she wasn't sure if it was intentional, either way it was working, her hair was up for the first time, her blue eyes had a sparkle Alex didn't see before.

"I guess you couldn't," Alex replied, she was trying not to show how nervous and excited she was.

"Can I," asked Noelle, "I mean kiss you?"

Alex leaned in with her eyes open; she wanted this moment to be special, they both waited for it so long. Noelle waited for it her whole life, she leaned in and closed her eyes. Their lips met. For Alex, it was everything she was hoping for, she calmed her nerves and enjoyed the moment.

Noelle tasted exactly like she thought she would. For Noelle, however, this was a new experience, she kissed girls in college during a drunken parties but it didn't lead anywhere. This, however, was so special. Alex's lips were soft, they tasted like peaches and summer. They kissed for a long time, one after another a passionate and hungry kiss.

The tension between them got even thicker. Noelle leaned in and gave Alex a big long hug; it felt so good to be in her arms, it felt like home. They heard someone moving around the parking lot and jumped in fear of getting caught. They looked at each other and started laughing. They both felt like teenagers doing something they shouldn't.

"You want to go back in?" Noelle asked. "I will stay here for a few minutes, fix my make-up and come up in a few."

"Sure," Alex answered, "before I go though." Alex put her hand on Noelle's face and gave her another short but intense kiss. "I will see you soon," she said with a smile on her face as she got out of the car.

Gabriela

The weekend went by quickly and Gabriela found herself in Karina's place during the week. This wasn't their normal routine, weekend get together but she was not going to complain. She brought a bag with a change of clothes for the morning so she can go straight into work. She knocked on the door, Karina opened it wearing a cute yellow apron.

"Quick, come in. I have to keep stirring." She rushed back into the kitchen. To Gabriela's surprise, she was making them dinner. The apartment smelled of fresh herbs and garlic.

"That's cute," said Gabriela. "I could get used to this, very domesticated. I haven't seen this side of you."

"Don't," laughed Karina. "You won't see this too often." She gave Gabriela a kiss on the cheek, she was covered in sauce and spices. "What's this?" She pointed at Gabriela's bag.

"My clothes for tomorrow," Gabriela replied as if this should be obvious.

"Oh, you're staying over?" Gabriela was confused by the question and Karina's tone.

"Should I not?" She asked.

"I suppose it is OK, it's just you never brought a bag before."

"Because I was never meant to stay, I thought…"

"It's ok," Karina interrupted her. "Honestly, it's fine. It just took me by surprise." She poured Gabriela a glass of red wine. "Come and sit you can watch me cook, take it all in as you will never see this again." She made a joke to lighten the mood.

"What is this?" Gabriela asked.

"The food, oh you will have to wait till it's ready."

"I don't mean the food." Gabriela felt uncomfortable to even attempt and start this conversation so quickly. She, however, really cared for Karina.

"This, I mean us."

"Oh you mean this not that," she made a joke again pointing at the pots and pans.

"Yes, I mean you and me."

"Well," Karina took a pause. She brushed her hand against her face leaving pieces of food on her forehead, in any other circumstances this would be quite comical, seeing her this way, such a perfect, god like beauty, today however she was fully, human.

"This is just us hanging out right?"

"Hanging out," Gabriela repeated. "OK, I come over, we have a great time. I stay, I go, I come back, is that what you want just to hang out?"

"I would like that yes, I think that's quite accurate? Don't you think?" In Karina's mind they reached consensus and understanding. This is all she had to offer and it was more than she offered anyone else. She liked Gabriela and wanted to play.

She knew from the start this is temporary and she will get bored soon. She however, liked her innocence.

"Is that cool?" She asked.

"And are you going to hang out with other people?" Gabriela asked.

"Sure, you can if you want to," Karina was trying to twist the conversation.

"I don't," Gabriela threw in quickly. "Are you?" Karina walked towards Gabriela and put her hands around her, she kissed her with those plump lips. They both knew it was designed to stop Gabriela from talking, from questioning her intentions.

"Look, I like you OK, but this is just who I am. I don't date for more than one maybe two dates. I'm not always here and I like to be free, to explore. I find a muse in every town it helps me with my work." – She took a sip of the wine.

"I don't want to be settled down, or to feel like I need to do something just because of someone else. I like you, I like to hang out with you and I like to spend time together. I even like when you stay over. I don't do that normally."

"But," she looked into Gabriela's eyes, "I don't think I can do more than that, is that a problem?"

Thousand thoughts went through Gabriela's head, this wasn't something she was used to. She was afraid she will be jealous, unsure of herself, that she won't be able to see or even imagine Karina with anyone else. But if those were the rules and the only way to see her, she was willing to at least try, for as long as it didn't hurt.

"Sure," she answered with a smile. Karina could see some sadness behind her eyes but she chose to focus on the smile.

"Good girl," she whispered into her ear before she gave it a little bite.

"Look, I don't know for how long I can do this on your terms but I will try to chill and just enjoy what we have," Gabriela added.

"All we have is this moment," Karina answered seductively, "and this moment is all we need. Now come help me finish this before it burns."

Gabriela had mixed fillings as to how this is going to affect her but she did indeed only have this moment so she decided to enjoy it. She had to travel to Italy for 3 months in order to sort out her visa and Italian passport, so maybe this was something that could work taking into consideration her own circumstances. She will enjoy what they have and move on when she has too.

She helped Karina finish the cooking and they had a relaxing dinner by the candle light. They talked and laughed, drank wine and once again she felt the world turned around just for them. She took in all of the beauty of this special moment.

Soon the only thing she will have are those memories. She didn't want to stain them with sadness or hope for something which might never happen. Karina stood up and took Gabriela by the hand.

"Come," she said. "I have dessert waiting inside."

Alex and Noelle

Alex came back to the office, trying her best to wipe the smile of her face and not to look too suspicious to her colleagues. Inside she was dancing. She didn't feel like this in a long time, the excitement and adrenaline were a dangerous mix. She saw Noelle going into her office a couple of minutes later.

She saw her talking to people and getting a cup of coffee before she walked into her office. She couldn't focus on work, the only thing she could focus on was the thought of Noelle's lips and the question on her mind of when she will be able to taste them again. After a while, her IM made a ping sound before she could even see it in the corner.

"Meet me in the bathroom," the words blinded Alex once again.

"Really?" she replied

"Really!" Noelle was getting bolder, Alex wasn't sure where this is going but she was happy to participate in whatever plan Noelle had. She waited a minute after she saw Noelle walking out of her office. It was getting late and the place wasn't busy.

Alex got up and walked pass a couple of people still working away, their heads down in their PC's unaware of what was going on around them. She smiled as the secret and sneaking around was making this even more exciting. She walked around the corner and opened the door to the toilet.

Two cubicles were open and the very last one was closed. She walked towards it and gently knocked on the door. Noelle unlocked it and let Alex in. The tight space forced them to stand very close to each other, not that either of them was going to complain. The tension between them was rather obvious.

"Hi," said Alex to break the silence.

"Hi back at you," said Noelle playfully. "Also keep it quiet and kiss me."

Alex leaned down and kissed Noelle just like her order commanded, their bodies now even closer to each other. Noelle slowly opened the buttons and took off her blouse. Alex couldn't believe what was happening. She stood in front of Noelle with her hands on her waist and her lips on Noelle's lips.

She turned Noelle around and leaned her body against hers, Noelle put one hand on the wall and the other one in Alex's hair. Alex was kissing her neck, tasting her skin while her hands travelled down Noelle's body. Noelle felt the heat rising between her legs just as when she was thinking about this moment, only so much better, so much more intense.

The passion was taking over their body's, they couldn't think clearly. Noelle turned around, Alex picked her up and placed her on top of her hips, she leaned her back against a wall, while kissing her neck and breasts. Noelle moved her arms and knocked the toilet paper dispenser, it fell on the ground and made a loud noise which shook them both and brought them back to reality.

"Oh fuck," said Alex as she gently placed Noelle's feet back on the ground.

"That's about right," Noelle licked her lips, she couldn't really speak.

"Not like this." Alex took a strand of hair away from Noelle's face. "I am staying in a hotel few minutes away from here."

"Take me there," that's all Noelle was able to whisper as she tried to catch her breath and find her blouse on the floor.

Alex parked the car at the back of the hotel, they went into the elevator blushing. Alex still wasn't sure how far this will go, she knew Noelle liked to be in control and she didn't want to take that comfort away from her. She wanted Noelle to feel safe. Alex put the key card in the door and let Noelle go in first.

The room was spacious. Alex's clothes gently placed around the place. She was immaculate, perfectionist and Noelle liked that about her, as she herself paid attention to details even the smallest ones. Alex opened a fridge and took out a small bottle of prosecco, she wanted to calm Noelle's nerves and give them both a minute to breath.

"Here," she handed the glass with a smile on her face, that innocent shy smile Noelle was already falling for.

"Thank you." Noelle took the glass and sculled it all down in one go.

"Oh OK," Alex laughed. She poured Noelle another one.

"I'm sorry." Noelle was blushing again.

"It's OK. Look, we don't have to do anything, we can just sit and talk," Alex smiled. "It's nice you know, just to have you here away from everyone, away from the world just you and me." Noelle gave Alex a long, tight hug.

"It is nice," she replied. "It feels like," she took a pause to collect her thoughts. She didn't want to say anything weird after all they only knew each other a couple of weeks. She couldn't deny that it felt right, when she was with Alex.

"It feels like home, when I'm in your arms." She smiled as she sat down to take her shoes off.

"I'm glad it does." Alex put on some music in the background she wanted both of them to feel relaxed. She sat down on the bed sipping her prosecco.

"Come here," she pointed at a spot next to her. "Sit down we can just relax and talk, tell me about your time away."

Noelle looked at Alex and with all of her courage blurred out.

"I can't let my clothes get messy now, can I?"

"No, I don't think you can, would you like me to get you a robe?" Alex asked politely trying not to make Noelle feel uncomfortable. She could feel fire in her veins as if it someone once again swapped her blood for gasoline.

"I think I will just have to take them off," she whispered seductively as she unzipped and slipped off her skirt. She continued to unbutton her blouse one by one until there was no more. She slipped it gracefully on the ground and stood in front of Alex, like a toned sculpture in white lingerie perfectly complementing her tanned body.

Alex moved to the edge of the bed. "That's wise," is all she was able to get out; she could feel her mouth getting dry and the heat rising between her legs. She never wanted anyone so much, the desire was burning in both of them. Alex put her hands on Noelle's hips, looking into her eyes she pulled her perfect body closer.

She kissed her stomach, smelled her skin. Noelle was playing with Alex's hair. It was new, exciting, uncharted for Noelle. It was something she was experiencing for the first time, yet it felt familiar. It felt as if she was supposed to be here her whole life, in this room with this beautiful, intriguing and cheeky woman she was so obsessed about.

Alex swiftly moved Noelle on to the bed and lay on top of her. They started kissing passionately, the hunger they both felt since the day they met was finally getting satisfied. Alex kissed Noelle's neck, her tongue and lips were travelling down Noelle's body. She kissed her breast, slowly and gently run her tongue around her nipples, they got harder and harder with each touch.

She kissed her stomach and slowly pulled her tongs down her legs. She looked into Noelle's eyes to make sure she is happy with what is about to happen next. Noelle smiled she leaned down and kissed Alex. Alex once again kissed every inch of Noelle's skin, from neck to her thighs.]

In her head, she wanted this to last longer, she wanted to play and tease and take her time, when it came to this moment she couldn't however stop herself. She gently spread Noelle's legs and put her head down, she slipped her tongue inside. Noelle moaned with pleasure. After a minute, she put her hand on Alex's head.

"Alex," she whispered.

Alex looked up making sure everything is OK. "Are you OK," she whispered.

"I'm fine." Noelle's eyes had a wild spark. "Can I try?" she asked blushing.

Alex smiled that beautiful smile. "Whatever feels right."

They were on their knees on the bed. Noelle slowly took off Alex's shirt, she opened the zip of her pants and seductively pushed them down until they ended up on the floor. She looked at Alex's blue bra and CK boxers, she liked what she was seeing more than she could ever imagine. She slowly took of her bra, putting her hand around Alex's breasts.

She kissed them, slowly and gently at first, she pulled Alex to the bottom of the bed and got down on her knees, she spread her legs and finally was able to taster her. For the first time in her life, she was able to fulfil the desire she didn't know was burning inside her. Her whole life she felt like something was missing, she finally realised what it was.

Gabriela

Gabriela got very little sleep last night as the dessert tasting took them a while. She went to the kitchen and grabbed a cup of coffee. Karina was already gone, all she left behind was a large pot of Italian coffee and a little note:

'See you Friday?'
Karina

Just one sentence, that's all, one promise of a good time and an opportunity to see her again, a chance to lose herself in this fairy-tale. How could she refuse. She took a shower and made her way into the coffee shop. After a while, her two favourite customers came in.

She hasn't seen them together in a week or so and seeing them made her happy. They looked different, she thought. They were giggling and smiling at each other. They seemed to not even notice anyone around them, as if the sun was shining only for them.

She knew that feeling and she was now sure there was something going on between them. That glow, that happiness, the way they looked at each other was exactly how she looked at Karina. Gabriela served them with a big smile on her face as they joked and laughed their energy was infectious.

She wondered if she will ever be able to share that with Karina. Just to enjoy their day together, go out talk to people show everyone what they feel for each other. Or maybe what she feels for her.

"Did you see that?" Gabriela asked her colleague while watching the two love birds until they disappeared in the little door leading upstairs.

"Saw what?" she replied confused.

"Them two," she pointed at the door. "Did you not see the sparks, come on the counter nearly went on fire." She laughed delighted with her witty comment. Her colleague looked her up and down.

"Are you OK? There is literally nothing going on here. You know life…"

"Is not an episode of the L word, I know I know," Gabriela cut in slightly annoyed at her colleagues inability to see what she saw.

"I'm telling you," she persisted, she looked into the cameras and saw them coming out from around the corner. "It took them a while," she whispered to herself. Maybe the cameras are a little slow, she thought and moved on with her day.

Alex and Noelle

Both cars pulled into the parking at nearly the same time. They got here unusually early and they were both in an exceptionally good moods. They walked to the café which was now becoming their spot and a morning routine.

Noelle was glowing, she felt as if she had a new lease on life. They ordered their morning magic potion and joked with the barista before taking stairs to the first floor where they could finish their morning ritual with a 30 minute sit down and chat. As they walked half way up the stairs, Alex looked around and stopped walking.

"No cameras," she told Noelle.

"I see." Noelle could read her mind, she pulled Alex closer and looked into her deep brown eyes. "I couldn't wait to see you this morning." Alex leaned her body against Noelle without a word, pushing her towards the wall. If it wasn't for the two hot coffees in her hand, she would probably reach under her dress.

"And what could you not wait for, to be exact." She smiled that cheeky smile showing off her dimples.

"Kiss me." Noelle pulled her even closer their lips met once again, it felt as if they belonged together. The kiss lasted until they heard the door opening downstairs. They laughed and rushed to their seats.

"How are you feeling?" Alex took off her jacket and placed it on the armchair across the couch.

"I'm great," Noelle smiled. She was playing with Alex's hair unaware of anyone or anything around them. "And you?"

"Well," Alex smiled. "I don't think I could be any better."

"Call me old fashioned," Noelle was blushing, "but would you like to be my girlfriend?"

Alex laughed, she didn't remember the last time anyone asked her that question, probably in a 5th grade if she had to recall such an occasion. Not in that way, not with such a cute, shy look. She wasn't thinking about Noelle's situation, in this moment it didn't seem important.

"I would like that very much," she answered with a hopeful look in her eyes.

"I think I'm a little obsessed with you," Noelle laughed.

"I can work with that."

"I have to go home after work today." Noelle all of a sudden seemed upset. "I need to."

"It's OK." Alex took her hand in her hand. "You do what you have to do."

"Thank you." She felt safe and unquestioned with Alex. People always had expectations of what she was supposed to do or say, with Alex it was easy, smooth, the connection they felt wasn't just physical it was so much more.

"I hope you didn't walk away from your relationship for me." Noelle's tone was a little bit more serious. "You know I can't promise anything."

"You should have thought about that before you asked me to be your girlfriend." Alex enjoyed messing with her. "It's ok," she smiled. "My relationship was over for a long time, meeting you just helped me see it and probably fast forwarded what future was going to bring anyway."

"That's good, I don't know," she took a pause.

"Stop, we don't know what future has in store for us, let's just enjoy what we have."

"Sounds good," a smile came back on Noelle's face. "You know there is a little get together after work tomorrow. I'm thinking we could join for a drink or two and then maybe leave early."

"And where would you like to go?" Alex asked.

"Take me to where you go, you know show me your world." She laughed.

"I'm afraid once I do, there is no going back," Alex was teasing her again.

"What if I don't want to go back?"

They finished their coffee and went into the office. They took extra few minutes on the stairs again to get a dose of each other's lips which had to sustain them till after work was finished and they can see each other in the parking lot. They both had to make an effort to hide the smile on their faces and dim down the glow if it was even possible.

The thoughts of a night together was making Alex happy, being with Noelle made her happier than she has ever been before. For Noelle, it felt as if a fog was lifted and for the first time she could see the world in its full beauty and glory.

Gabriela

Friday came quickly to Gabriela's delight as she was able to see Karina, escape her reality and enter this amazing fairy tale for another night. She felt brave in the morning and decided to text and just be forward with what she wanted.

"Hey, should I pack an over weekend bag? I am off and don't have plans so was thinking maybe I stay the whole weekend?"

Send. She regretted the decision as soon as she pressed the button. She didn't, however, want to delete it and come across, cowardly. The three moving dots seemed to be taking forever, the word 'typing' was painful to watch.

"Sure."

A quick and painless reply came back.

"How about we head out tonight? Might be fun?"

Another text followed. Gabriela wasn't a fan of night clubs or pubs or anything that meant socialising or being out in public making small talk with strangers but she was willing to try it out with Karina. Seeing the possibly secret couple every day at work made her feel a little envious, she wanted to show Karina off for the world to see.

"Sure"

Another quick reply. Gabriela was excited to see what the night will bring. She knew soon she has to go away for a couple of months so she might as well make the most of her time here. Or anytime she had left with her princess charming.

Her shift was over; Gabriela ran home to pack some things and headed over to Karina's. She was happy and excited by the thought of a long weekend and a bit more fun than she was used to. She arrived at the apartment around 9 and found Karina ready to head out into the night. Karina was in great form, she seemed more excited than usual.

"What are you so happy about?" Gabriela asked with a hint of suspicion.

"What are you so grumpy about?" Karina responded teasingly. Gabriela laughed unsure of what is happening.

"Come here, we have to celebrate," said Karina pouring them both a glass of champagne.

"What are we celebrating," Gabriela still wasn't sure what's happening.

"I made a big sale today; the whole collection, all gone." She responded with a big smile.

"Congratulations," Gabriela lifted the glass. "So what's next?"

"What's next?" The question amused Karina. "Next we celebrate," she moved closer and gently kissed Gabriela's neck. "Then we celebrate some more," she moved around and kissed the other side. "And then," she took a sip of the champagne, "and then I will get out there again and create another one." She smiled, pretty delighted with her idea.

"That sounds awesome." Gabriela was happy for her, she didn't want to mention that she needs to go away for a while. It didn't seem to matter as their relationship was casual and this sort of made it easier. Karina won't be here either.

"So," she continued, "where are you thinking of going?" Karina smiled.

"Tonight I'm going to town and after that south of the border," she looked Gabriela up and down and licked her lips. She was in great mood, a friskier mood it seemed like. Gabriela wasn't sure what the night is going to bring but she found herself more adventures in her company.

South of the border sounds good.

Alex and Noelle

The work day was finally coming to a finish; normally Fridays go quick this one however seemed to last forever. Everyone was getting ready for the after work drinks in a nearby pub. Noelle went home to change and leave the car outside she was going to come down a little later, Alex didn't expect anything less than a big entrance.

She also drove down to her hotel and left the car in the parking, showered got changed and hoped in a taxi to the venue. Even though they were not going to stay there long, dinner and a few drinks not to raise suspicion every minute seemed like an hour. Noelle was so close, even though she was literally at arm's length, she might as well have been a million miles away with all these people around.

They threw each other a hungry glance every now and then, making sure no one is catching them in the act. Alex never thought it will be so hard to stay away from someone, she enjoyed looking at Noelle. Despite her being deep in a conversation Noelle would throw Alex a quick glance back quite often, as if to make sure her object of desire is still there.

Couple of hours into the night, everyone was getting a little tipsy and it seemed like the best time to leave. No one was paying them any mind. They left separately and met around the corner where they got a taxi to the club.

"I have never been there," Noelle said with an innocent enthusiasm.

"You have never been where," Alex was taking pleasure in teasing her, she couldn't wait to be in a safe space, where they can just enjoy each other.

"You know," Noelle was blushing. "Your kind of club."

"My kind of club, is it." Alex laughed. "You straight girls are all the same."

"Excuse me?" Noelle didn't seem impressed with the comment.

"Relax, just enjoy the freedom."

The taxi pulled outside the 'George', the biggest and possibly only gay night club in the city and they slowly moved towards the door. It must have been close to 10 but the front door was still open. As soon as they walked in, Alex was able to really relax, that familiar feeling of being 'home' hit her as soon as the door closed behind them.

The music, some people already dancing and others chatting around the bar, the lights, the sense of freedom and liberation always made her feel good. She was glad she was the one to introduce Noelle to this amazing community. Noelle looked back making sure Alex is behind her. Her eyes were full of wonder and excitement as if she was a child walking for the first time into a candy store.

"You OK?" Alex took Noelle's hand. Noelle shivered at first but realised quickly she can be herself. No one here knows her, no one will judge her, no one knows she left a perfect marriage and two kids back in France just to be here.

"I'm great," she whispered into Alex's ear as they moved towards the bar.

Into You by Ariana Grande was playing in the background; they couldn't imagine a better choice of song for their circumstances. The secrecy of this affair was making it so much more exciting, for Noelle anyway, Alex wanted it to be her every day. They drank all night, they danced, they kissed like a pair of teenagers and bounced of everyone walking pass.

They talked to strangers, shared their story and desire with anyone willing to listen. Noelle enjoyed how they looked together, even more so how people looked at them. She saw the short and long gazes people threw towards her girlfriend and towards her, and she enjoyed knowing in this very moment Alex was hers and only hers.

Noelle for the first time in her life felt free, she felt like she doesn't have to be anything for anyone, she can just be herself and do what she wants to do, which is to be with Alex. Dance, laugh, feel her body against her own. Time was passing so quickly she didn't want the night to end. She knew, however, this might be her only opportunity to be with Alex till the morning.

"Take me home."

"OK," Alex replied with a smile on her face. "Whatever my lady wants."

"She is right you know."

"Who?" Alex asked curiously.

"Our girl Ariana." Noelle kissed Alex and whispered into her ear, "I always get what I like just like she says."

They arrived in a hotel few minutes later. They fell into the room driven by desire they both felt for the first time, and for the first time they were able to indulge fully. Alex put on music and poured them a glass of prosecco she left in a cooler earlier that night.

"I could get used to this." Noelle said playfully taking the glass from her hand.

"Maybe that's the point." Alex was as quick and witty, Noelle liked that about her.

"I will be back in a min." Noelle whispered on her way to the bathroom.

After a couple of minutes, she walked out of the toilet wearing red heels and lingerie in a matching shade. Alex could feel her mouth dry out within seconds. She imagined this so many times, the reality was however, so much better than fantasy. She sat on the bottom of the bed and let Noelle be in control, she will play the game for as long as she can before she explodes.

Noelle walked over and seductively spread Alex's legs with her knee. She turned around and bend down just to slowly get back up. Alex put her hands on Noelle's waist and tried to pull her towards herself, Noelle however, was not finished with the show. She pushed Alex back and stepped away.

She put her hands on the wall and moved her hips right and left slowly into the rhythm of the music. Alex couldn't take it. She pulled Noelle closer and reached between her legs. She pulled Noelle's head down and kissed her neck, bit her ear and run her tongue on Noelle's skin.

She stood up and turned Noelle around placing her hands back on the wall. She knew the tables have turned and she was now the one in control. She let Noelle arch her back and lean against her as she reached down between her legs. Noelle couldn't do anything other than surrender.

It must have been 5 am by the time Alex and Noelle fell asleep, wrapped in nothing but each other's bodies.

Gabriela

Gabriela and Karina got to the club around 11. They got in through the side door without having to queue. Gabriela started to enjoy the perks that came from dating Karina. The place was busy as usual, the dance floor full, queue to the bathroom and crowd to the bar just a usual Friday night, any night really.

The choices were scarce maybe three, four gay bars at best. She wasn't a big fan of the scene or any bars really but she enjoyed her time with Karina regardless of where they went. Karina took Gabriela's hand and brought her to an empty table in the corner.

"I didn't know you can reserve tables here?" Gabriela said.

"Oh darling." her innocence seemed to amuse Karina. "You can do whatever you want when you're, well, me."

Gabriela never saw this side of Karina, she was normally very confident but this was different. This was more borderline of 'I can do what I want when I want.' Gabriela was curious to see what happens.

The drinks seem to be arriving every so often, as if bottles of champagne just appeared on the table out of nowhere. Anytime they finished one, another one was placed down. Gabriela wasn't much of a dancer but Karina didn't mind. She amused herself and grooved to the music.

Any music really, from the sophisticated sounds of jazz and classical tunes at home to Pop and RnB in the club. She had that lightness about her, grace and class not many possess.

"So, which one would you like to try today?" Karina asked Gabriela out of nowhere

"Which one I would like to do what now?" Gabriela wasn't sure what was happening, which once again seemed to be a source of amusement for her date.

"Which girl would you like to bring home?" Karina rephrased the question.

"I am coming home with you, no?" Gabriela still seemed not to grasp what Karina was asking.

"You are with me at least once a week, right?" Karina asked. "Today we celebrate, we play so I will ask one more time," she took a sip from her glass and looked around. "Which one would you like to bring home with us, so we can play?" She looked at Gabriela who was distracted by someone at the bar.

"Well, well, didn't take you long. Good choice on both accounts but which one are you thinking? Or are you thinking both?"

"What?" Gabriela asked once again confused.

"You are staring at the two girls right? I should say two women, nice choices." Karina pointed at a couple at the bar. They were wrapped around each other, fresh love, she thought.

"I'm not sure if they will be interested, they seem like they have all they want." Their passion and body language were quite telling.

"Oh no," Gabriela laughed. "They are customers, they come to my work. Every morning for the last while they come in and stay upstairs for a bit, they always laugh and giggle and I just knew there is something going on." Karina laughed amused by the story.

"You will have to tell me about this later," she brought Gabriela's attention back to her question. "Any preference as to who is coming home with us?"

"No," Gabriela answered looking Karina straight in the eyes. Those almond like, black eyes she couldn't resist. "It is your playground, your rules, you pick the playmate."

Karina laughed. "OK then."

Two hours later, Karina, Gabriela and a cute blond very femme girl came out of the club. They got in a taxi and arrived in the apartment 10 minutes later. Gabriela wasn't sure if she wanted to be a part of this. Of whatever this was going to be.

She has never done this and had feelings for Karina even though they were supposed to keep things casual. Karina was happy, she was celebrating and the world was her oyster. The elevator door opened and Karina took out the keys to open the apartment door.

"Gabriela, would you mind opening a bottle? We will wait in the bedroom," she commanded as she showed their new friend a way in. To Gabriela's surprise, they didn't go to the room they normally stay in. They went past the bathroom to the door she has never noticed before. She was here so many times yet she never bothered to ask what's there.

She put three glasses on a tray and popped the champagne. She had a slight smile on her face as she walked into the room. It had a massive king size bed and silky sheets, the light was dimmed it was,

"A sex room?" Gabriela asked Karina.

"Oh, I wouldn't call it that." Karina laughed. She took a glass for herself and handed one to their guest. The girl stood in front of Karina and Gabriela and started kissing Karina's neck.

"So," Karina looked at Gabriela. "You want to play?" Gabriela put down her glass and kissed the other side of Karina's neck. Karina smiled and took a step back.

"No," she said as she sat down on a large, red armchair. "You play and I watch."

"You just watch?" Gabriela asked.

"I watch until I want to join." Karina smiled, a look of satisfaction came over her face. She took a sip of the champagne. The game was hers and so where the rules.

Gabriela looked at the girl and kissed her lips, unzipped her dress and started slowly slipping it off looking into Karina's eyes watching them from across the room.

Gabriela got quite tipsy and passed out in her bedroom shortly after they were finished. It was down to Karina to order a taxi and say goodbye to her new friend or rather brief encounter. She was too eager for Karina's liking but amused her tonight and that was the sole purpose of this evening.

She walked to the bedroom and stood in the door for a little while just looking at Gabriela. She was so innocent, so beautiful. Karina smiled thinking about their time together. She was surprised Gabriela was so open to the new experience. She didn't think she will want to go through with it.

She looked at Gabriela and the moon shimmering on her skin. She took out her camera and took a couple of pictures. I will show her tomorrow, I'm sure she won't mind. She thought as she lied next to Gabriela, she brushed off a curly lock of her hair and kissed her forehead before falling asleep next to her.

Noelle

Noelle woke up to a sound of rain bouncing of the window. It took her few minutes to open her eyes and realise where she is. Alex was sound asleep next to her. Noelle didn't want to wake her, she took her time and watch Alex sleep. She was so peaceful, so at ease exactly how Noelle felt around her.

It was as if all of a sudden the voice in her head stopped, the constant vortex of thoughts and questions was now silent. She was herself, she didn't have to pretend or behave in a way she thought she should, in a way people expected her to. Here, with Alex she just was, and who she was she very much enjoyed. She fell in love not just with Alex but also with the person she was becoming around her.

Alex was confident, charming and brave. Noelle was brave when it came to taking risks, opening business and going for what she wanted professionally, she wasn't brave when it came to her needs and desires, when it came to that she very much conformed to society's norms. Her conventional life was everything she knew, and maybe Liam made it easy.

Easy to be with him, easy to stay, he was easy to love and he took care of all the things she didn't want to think about. He enabled her to be who she wants to be without worrying about the life's obstacles and worries. He was an amazing man, she started wondering was he the man for her. Liam was warm and caring, he was loving and he didn't push her, he never asked for anything not even for sex.

Once things slowed down, she was coming up with excuses until he just stopped asking, stopped trying to make suitable circumstances and she was quite happy about that. She never quite understood why she is finding it hard to be intimate with this amazing man, with her own husband. The answer to that finally came.

Noelle looked at Alex again, she realised she was deep in thought; this time she didn't want that, all she wanted is to be here with Alex. Something about

Alex made her feel comfortable, liberated, free she wanted this feeling to last. She couldn't wait for Alex to wake, all she wanted in this moment was to taste her skin, and to feel that sweetness between her legs.

She didn't know when and if she will have a chance to stay over and wake up next to her lover, her girlfriend. She smiled as the thought of having a girlfriend crossed her mind. She never thought her life will take such an amazing turn, she never thought she will feel so alive.

Alex moved and opened her eyes. She didn't anticipate finding Noelle next to her, just peacefully staring, observing. It seemed Noelle was just that, an observer and participant in Alex's life. She knew she wanted to be more, she wanted it to be her life, her reality.

"Hey," Alex whispered.

"Hey," Noelle replied playfully. She leaned towards Alex and kissed her.

"Mhmmm," moaned Alex. "I could get used to that."

"I'm sure you could." Noelle picked up a flyer lying on the bed side table. "Breakfast?" she asked.

"I would love one, but hey, maybe we will go out? Walk, park, brekky by the river?"

Noelle loved the idea, she would love nothing more than to go out, hold hands and show Alex off to everyone. She would love to spend time with her, all the time in the world. She was, however, afraid someone will see them. She needed some time to pass to get used to the idea she is with a woman and figure out what to do with her marriage before she goes out in a bright day light, in public.

"Can we stay in the room?" She asked. "I am not ready to share you with the world."

"Of course," Alex answered. "The world can wait."

Noelle came home that afternoon. She wanted to stay with Alex so bad she knew however, she needs to prepare both her home and herself for her family's arrival. She missed her boys so much, she missed Liam too, not in the husband-wife sort of a way. She knew she loves him she just didn't know what sort of love it was, they were partners, they completed each other in life.

It was becoming clearer to her that kind of partnership just wasn't enough, she wanted to feel fire, desire, she wanted to wake up next to Alex not just occasionally but each and every day. She took a long shower as if to wash the infidelity of her skin. She will have to put on a mask and pretend everything is

OK, an art she mastered over the years before she knew who she really was and what she desired.

She knew she will have to talk to Liam. The feelings she had for Alex were not going anywhere, if anything they were getting stronger. She loved the way she walked, the way she danced, the way people looked at them when they entered the club, the fun they had and most of all she loved the way their bodies connected and what Alex was able to do to her, something no one else did.

She cannot give up this connection, she has given up so much to be where and who she is but no more. Noelle put a soft, cashmere robe around her perfectly toned body and walked to the boys' room. She smelled their blankets, she didn't realise how much she missed their little faces. They will be OK, she thought, she will do whatever she can to make sure they are OK.

She sat on the bed and started crying. She felt torn between being a mother and her family and the woman she was discovering was underneath it, all along.

Alex

"Another surprise," Michelle smiled. "Once again I didn't think I will see you."

"I know," Alex replied. "I'm sorry I think I would like to keep coming, just to check in with myself."

"That's perfectly fine. What would you like to talk about today?" Michelle asked taking out the notebook.

"First of all thank you for fitting me in," said Alex. "I'm moving today, I found a room close to the office, so that's a good start and a nice change from the hotel room." She smiled a cheeky, dreamy smile.

"Something on your mind?" Michelle noticed the change in Alex's expression.

"Noelle was with me last night. She stayed over."

"How did it feel?"

"Good," a big smile covered Alex's face. "Great actually."

"Tell me more about it?"

"You know I never felt this comfortable with anyone before. We laugh, we talk and we are so into each other, it's amazing."

"How do you feel? Not We."

"I feel amazing, I never thought I can have that in my life."

"And," Michelle paused, she didn't want to overstep but she wanted to make sure Alex is aware of the situation she is in. "Is Noelle living at home?" She tried to ask as gentle as possible.

"Yes she is, with her husband and two kids if that's what you're asking." Alex was calm answering the question.

"And how does that make you feel?" Michelle was able to continue she was surprised and pleased with Alex's openness.

"I mean, it's not ideal. At the same time I knew the risk when I was going into this, affair, relationship whatever you want to call it."

"What do you want to call it?" Michelle interrupted.

"I don't want to call it anything," Alex smiled she came across very peaceful and happy, completely different person to their first session. "I enjoy what we have, me and Noelle. I enjoy every moment and when she's not with me, I can't wait to see her again. It has helped me so much, this situation. It helped me realise my relationship was no longer working, it made clear what I want in life, how I want my relationships to look like. Also."

Alex paused to collect her thoughts. "It's nice you know, to see yourself through someone else's eyes, to realise what you have to offer and how amazing being with someone might feel like, someone who enjoys your company."

"You didn't feel that before?"

"No, not really, my ex always wanted her friends around. She thought people who go out on their own are boring and don't have friends, she didn't want to be just with me, I wouldn't mind a balance."

"And what do you want? Seems like at the moment it's the complete opposite".

"It is, it feels like we can't get enough of each other."

"Well, you seem happy. Are you OK with the fact she is married?" Michelle felt comfortable to ask the direct question.

"I mean, of course I would love for us to have a future together, to have a life and I think we will. But I wouldn't push Noelle to do anything she's not ready for. I signed up for this knowing the risk and I'm OK with whatever happens. I needed this and I am grateful for how it changed my life."

"Good to hear." Michelle was glad Alex is doing OK and she realises what she is doing. "Just don't forget you changed your life."

"I guess I did," Alex smiled. "I chose happiness and the rest just followed. I spend hours just thinking about that perfect relationship and how should it feel. Nothing quite felt right in the past." She looked at Michelle and smiled. "Now, however, everything feels right."

Alex came out of the office smiling. She was in great form and was really looking forward to see what the future holds. She hopped in the car and drove to the hotel to collect her things and bring them to the new apartment.

She needed to go back to the house she once shared with Niamh and collect the remaining of her clothes and anything that belonged to her, but that was a task for another day.

Gabriela

"Is she gone?" Gabriela whispered as soon as Karina's eyes opened.

"Is who gone?" Karina seemed confused.

"Your Blondie?" Gabriela wasn't amused by Karina's answer.

"Of course she is gone. I don't let people stay over," she gave Gabriela a long cold look. "Well, except you I guess."

"So that's it?" Gabriela was trying to make sense of the experience and understand the pattern.

"That's it what?" It seemed Karina was playing another one of her games. "Yes that's it we will never see her again. Happy now?" she added.

"I guess. I kind of hoped we can make it a regular thing." Gabriela was now the one playing games.

"Really?"

"No, not really," Gabriela laughed and sat on top of Karina, she put her hands behind her head and kept her down. "I would like for us not to do it again. If that's ok," she added.

"OK." Gabriela was surprised by Karina's answer.

"OK?"

"Yes, we don't have to do it again. I mean I don't want to make you feel uncomfortable." Gabriela knew this isn't the real reason but she was going to take it.

"Great, not that I was uncomfortable…"

"Oh no," Karina cut her off. "You seemed very comfortable, as if you have done it before even." Gabriela refused to answer that, she wanted Karina to be curious, a little jealous even. Maybe just maybe there is a chance Karina is starting to feel something for her and she was not going to let that bubble burst. Not today, not ever.

"Shower before breakfast?" Gabriela asked playfully.

"Oh, someone is getting cocky here, why do you think there will be breakfast?"

"Well." Gabriela felt in control for the first time since they met. "Isn't there always?" She laughed as she run into the bathroom and turned on the water. "Come on join me," she stuck her head through the door. "Let's be good to the planet and conserve water, shall we?"

"Take your time," Karina answered. "I need to get ready for the sale next week and have a lot to do." She walked towards the bathroom and looked at Gabriela's body in the shower. "I think it's better if you go after the shower, hope that's OK?" She added, yet they both knew she didn't really care.

Something changed in Karina's voice. Gabriela once again felt like an intruder; she felt she crossed a boundary she didn't know existed.

"Ok," she answered as she turned off the shower and covered her body with a soft, white towel. She put on her clothes and went out to the living room. She found Karina on the balcony with a cup of fresh coffee. This time however there was no coffee for her.

"Is everything OK?" Gabriela reached out and touched Karina's back. "Did I do something?" Karina didn't look at her she just coldly answered.

"No, you haven't done anything. Look, we had a good time, it's just not me. I don't like commitment and this feels like it's turning into one." She gave Gabriela a subtle smile.

"OK," Gabriela was surprised. She wasn't sure what has happened within the last 30 minutes and what brought this upon. "Look, it doesn't have to be." Gabriela tried to salvage some sort of unwritten agreement.

"I am going away at the end of September, for at least 3 months. I need to go to Italy to take care of some legal stuff. Maybe we can at last see each other till then?" She didn't want to give this up, not just yet.

"Sure," Karina remained cold. "Maybe we can."

"OK." Gabriela wasn't sure she was getting anywhere. "Would you like me to stay or come over next weekend."

"I will call you," Karina answered. "Look, you're a nice girl and I like you, it's just not who I am. I don't do this, weekends, staying over, breakfast; I don't do any of it. I don't do commitment and it feels you are getting too comfortable."

"Wow!" Gabriela didn't know how to respond, in truth she was getting quite comfortable. "I'm sorry you feel that way."

"It's not your fault." Karina looked at Gabriela's brown, sad eyes. She put her hand on Gabriela's face. "You are a good kid, we are just from two different worlds you and me." Gabriela felt hurt and angry. She, however, knew this isn't going to last forever, she just wanted it to last a little bit longer.

"I am going to leave Dublin next weekend," Karina continued. "I won't be around for a couple of weeks. I don't think there is a point to keep doing this. I don't want to hurt you, kid."

Gabriela went back into the apartment without saying anything. She packed her clothes and collected anything she might have left. Deep down, she knew she won't be here again. Her fairy tale was over, there won't be a happy ever after, not for them. Not now, maybe not ever.

"Where are you going?" Gabriela asked on her way to the door.

"Greece I think, maybe south Italy after I'm not sure yet. I will go wherever the inspiration takes me."

"Call me if you get to Italy, I might be there at the same time." Gabriela tried to hold on to some glimpse of hope that maybe they will see each other again.

"I will." Karina gave her a kiss on the cheek and gently stroked her hand. "I hope you're ok," she added.

"I'll be fine, I just." Gabriela took a pause. "I didn't see this coming. Not so quickly."

"I know," Karina's voice was now much softer. "I'm sorry, kid."

Gabriela opened the door and walked out to the hall. There was so many things she wanted to say, she however couldn't think of one that will in any way help the situation. Pleading, asking, begging she didn't want to do any of it. She knew this day would come and she knew she was on borrowed time.

She didn't feel good enough for Karina. She was angry at herself for letting her in, for letting her heart fall for her. She always thought the trip to Italy will be the end of this as Karina would not wait for her, she wouldn't wait for anyone. As she walked down the hall towards the elevator she saw the girl from the coffee shop.

Alex was her name, she thought. She looked up and gave her a little smile, that's all she was able to muster.

"Hi." She nodded.

"Hi," Alex replied. "Are you OK? You look upset." Alex was a kind soul and it seemed Gabriela needed kindness.

"I'm fine," as the words came out of Gabriela's mouth an uncontrollable stream of tears poured out of her eyes.

"Come in." Alex took her by the hand and invited her into the apartment.

Gabriela didn't have a chance to talk or explain she found herself in the arms of the stranger she only knew from her work. She cried what felt like a stream of never ending tears.

Alex

It has taken Alex two rounds of coffee and camomile tea before the Barista girl calmed down. My first day in this place, Alex thought, and already I'm a part of some drama.

"Do you want to talk?" Alex asked with kindness in her voice.

"I don't know," Gabriela took a sip of her tea. "Thank you," she added with big, teary brown eyes.

"It's OK." Alex was very understanding "We all go through things in life, we all need a helping hand sometimes, an arm to cry on if you like."

"I guess we do." Gabriela was now in a much better shape, she needed a good cry. She felt, however, she has no more tears left.

"So, boy drama?" Alex was doing her best to keep it light, it worked as Gabriela smiled.

"More like girl drama," she replied.

"I see," Alex had a feeling but she didn't want to make assumptions.

"You know," Gabriela wasn't sure if it's OK but she shared her thoughts anyway. "I saw you last night. In the club." Alex shifted in her seat.

"Did you now," they both smiled as if now they were a part of a secret.

"I did," she continued. "With your friend," Gabriela blushed. "Well, more than a friend I guess." She added.

"It's complicated," Alex crossed her hands across her chest. Gabriela didn't practice for a while but even without a psychology diploma one would know this is making her uncomfortable.

"I'm sorry," she felt uneasy and guilty. Alex was kind to her and she didn't mean to make her feel uncomfortable in her own home.

"It's ok," Alex smiled. "It's not your fault. Now tell me why were you crying? Anything I can do to help."

"Break up." Gabriela was doing her best not to break down again. "Well, not really a break up more like inevitable."

"Some things are just not meant to be. We need to enjoy the little moments in life and everyone we meet teaches us a lesson. Don't look at it as something bad, be grateful for what you had and move on."

"That seems reasonable." Gabriela understood what Alex meant. It was, however, hard to apply the logic in this very moment.

"I know it's hard to think in those lines when your suffering," Alex added nearly as if she could read her mind. "Give yourself time, but focus on gratitude not on the pain."

The advice was good and Gabriela knew she needs to shift her focus. It will take a while but she was going to be OK. She walked home after leaving Alex's place and went straight to bed. She didn't care it was early.

She wanted to sleep, wake up the next morning and realise this was just a bad dream. Only a nightmare that would be gone once she opens her eyes and not an actual chapter in her life. The next morning, however, felt even more painful.

She started to organise her documents and refocus her attention on to what she needed to do. She made a to-do list and booked tickets to make sure she stays focused on her future. No more distractions.

Noelle

The choice between doing what's right and what feels right was eating Noelle up. She looked at the address she got from Alex and the scheduled time for the arrival of her family's flight. She has about two hours to get to the airport, is it enough time to drive to town, see her lover and then get to the airport and collect her family.

Is it enough time to transition from a wild, passionate woman to a mother and wife. She wished those two things could go hand in hand, however she didn't know if they ever could. One thing she knew for certain she was not willing to give herself up anymore.

She gave up so much and she was not going to let Alex slip through her fingers. She had to do anything in her power to keep her. To keep and nurture what they had. Even if it costed her the picture perfect marriage and life she created. She picked up the phone and rang Alex.

"Hey, gorgeous," Alex answered promptly.

"I miss you," the longing in Noelle's voice was easy to read.

"Well, what are we going to do about it?"

"Can you come down?"

"Where would you like me to come?" Alex asked happy to hear Noelle is taking initiative once again.

"There is a park not far from my home, come and we can go for a walk. I will have 30 minutes before I have to." Noelle took a pause, she didn't want to spoil this moment. Alex didn't ask. She never pushed, she never asked for an explanation.

"Sure. I will be down in 20 minutes, that OK?"

"That's perfect."

They both arrived in the parking lot of the large park at the same time. Sea on one side of the street and St Anne's park on the other. It was more like a groomed forest than a park. It was large and had some secluded spots. You didn't have to be seen if you didn't want to.

Alex got out of the car and waited for Noelle in the agreed spot. She saw Noelle skipping towards her, her hair was up and the shape of her perfect body visible through the tight black gym outfit she was wearing.

"Casual Sunday, I see," Alex made an observation.

"Casual weekends you mean." Noelle leaned and kissed Alex on the lips; it seemed she didn't care who's around and who can see them. She wanted to feel Alex, even just her lips. She took Alex by the hand and they walked towards the trees.

"How are you?" Noelle asked. "How's your apartment?"

"It's awesome," Alex replied, she seemed happy. "I would like you to see it sometime."

"I would love that." Noelle was also happy and eager. "I'm going to talk to Liam."

"About?" Alex wasn't sure what Noelle meant, she however, hoped it was what she thought.

"About us, I mean about me. About me being." She took a pause to find the right words. "Gay I guess."

"Don't label yourself." Alex didn't want Noelle to jump to conclusions or do anything she wasn't ready for. "Don't do anything on my account."

"I am not." Noelle stopped walking and turned her face towards Alex. "I can no longer live a lie. Not after meeting you, not after what we feel towards each other. Alex…" She took Alex's hands in her hands and looked her deep in the eyes.

"I love you, Alex."

Alex's heart stopped. She knew she fell for Noelle but she didn't know if Noelle will ever feel the same way, if she will ever get the courage to say those words. "I love you too," Alex whispered back. They kissed under the trees with a gust of wind blowing around them.

In this very moment, only they knew what they feel for each other. In the whole world, 7 billion people they were the only 2 souls sharing this secret only them and the wind as their witness.

After a short walk, Noelle had to leave. She had to go back to her home and pretend everything is OK. Pretend until the right time, the time to talk to her husband and take steps towards their future. For now, the random encounters in the park, morning coffees and after work drinks had to be enough.

Alex knew it will have to sustain her till they can take it to the next step. She came back to her apartment and was longing for Noelle. She sat on her bed and wished Noelle was there with her. She wanted to go to sleep wrapped around her body and wake up next to her.

She didn't know, however, when or if this will happen. She had hoped and hope was all she had. Alex opened Pinterest, she wanted to leave something for Noelle. She picked a beautiful sunrise with caption.

'The purpose of our lives is to be happy.'
She scrolled some more and picked another one:
'Sometimes life is about risking everything for a dream no one can see but you.'

She wanted to leave something to let her know she is thinking of her and she loves her.

Noelle got to the airport and took a quick glance at her phone just as the plane was landing. She was excited to see the boys, she also felt pain as it meant she won't be able to see Alex, not as often as she would like anyway. She opened Pinterest and what she saw brought a smile on her face. She quickly scrolled through some pins to make sure she leaves something for Alex.

'That person who enters your life out of nowhere, and suddenly means the world to you.'

She smiled as she knew this is exactly how they both feel, the peace, the calmness she felt while with Alex could not be expressed with words. She wanted to get lost in that again but it will have to wait till tomorrow. The boys run out of the door and it brought a tear to Noelle's eyes.

Karina

Karina didn't do much after Gabriela left her apartment that Saturday afternoon. She spend the whole weekend drinking wine and thinking about what happened. Not just that day but over the last few weeks. Normally reserved and cold, she took down her guard and let someone in.

She knew they don't have a future together but she didn't want that anyway. She was entertained, she felt comfortable and she liked the young girl. Her youth and innocence reminded Karina of herself a long time ago. She didn't know when the situation stopped being comfortable for her, something changed within seconds and she could no longer enjoy her company.

It must have been the way she was willing to try anything, the way she was willing to do things against her own, better judgement just to satisfy Karina. She didn't like that, she didn't want that for anyone. It's the strength that Gabriela was lacking, the strength she was so attracted to.

She never met anyone as strong as her, as independent as her. She could seduce anyone with just one look and that person would lose themselves in her eyes and between her sheets. And like a magic spell she would have them in her control. This could only, however, amuse her for so long, that was the reason she didn't commit or didn't settle, didn't try a relationship.

She knew if she was ever to try, it would have to be someone special, someone not just as strong as her but someone, somewhat immune to her charm. She was yet to meet a woman like that. She was done with contemplation and wanted a little entertainment. She send a text and went into the bathroom for a quick shower, she got dressed in skinny jeans, black tight blouse and leather jacket.

Her perfect black hair was up in a bun and with her caramel skin and high cheek bones; she didn't need much make up. She always looked flawless, just like her pictures. She was herself a piece of art. She took her camera and went downstairs, a car was waiting, the driver without a word took her to where she wanted to go.

The door to the club opened and a gentleman in a black suit brought her around the back to the private room. The walls were painted dark red, same colour as a large leather sofa in the middle of the room. The light was dimmed just like she asked and a bottle of champagne on ice placed precisely in the middle of a round table next to the sofa.

The black curtain opened exposing a large mirror, the colours of the room bounced of the silver pole in the middle of a little stage. The waiter came in quietly.

"Is there anything you would like?"

"Another glass please, and bring 2nd bottle in 30 minutes," Karina answered without even looking at him.

"Right away." The glass appeared on the table within seconds. He closed the door behind him.

Karina took off her jacket, she poured two glasses of champagne and relaxed into the sofa. A female voice appeared from behind the curtain.

"You know we can't drink during work." A tall, tattooed brunette teased her.

"As if it's the first time you break the rules," Karina answered confidently. She passed 2nd glass to the dancer. "Cheers," she whispered.

"Cheers," the girl replied.

"Now dance," Karina commanded. She liked being in control. And from all the games she enjoyed playing, this was by far her favourite.

"Haven't seen you in a while." Brunette put the glass back on the table and touched Karina's face. She lifted her chin up so she could see her eyes. "Are you cheating on me?" She laughed.

"Do I pay you for talking?" Karina was in total control.

The brunette walked towards the stage. She got on and grasped the pole with her two hands. The music started playing. She moved her body flawlessly to the rhythm using the pole as if it was a part of her. Karina sunk in the sofa, she drank her champagne and enjoyed the show in silence.

After a while, she took her camera and started taking pictures. She took some from a far and then zoomed into the different parts of her body. The colours, the dimmed lights, it was perfect. In the past, she came here rather often.

She always took pictures but never published any of them, even though some of them were her finest work, they were only hers, they were her private collection. She put down her camera and finished the first bottle of champagne. The second one arrived shortly after. She knew from now on they will not be disturbed. Not until she is done.

"Come here," she ordered. The brunette came down from the stage and stood in front of Karina in her perfect, black leather lingerie. Karina was trying to reach out and touch her but she slapped her hand.

"You know you can't do that," Raven said playfully.

"What else can I not do?" Karina asked seductively. "I definitely shouldn't do that then," she turned the girl around and slapped her perfectly shaped ass.

"No, you should definitely not have done that." The girl smiled. Her black long hair coming down on Karina's face, she sat on top of Karina and put her hands on her body. Karina slowly opened her bra. "Then that's out of the question," she continued the game.

"Well, that's definitely out of the question." Raven grabbed Karina by her face and looked into her eyes. "Who's the girl you were out with last night?" She more so demanded the answer.

"She's no one," Karina answered moving her head from the grasp. "No one you need to bother yourself with."

"Well, obviously," she laughed. "You wouldn't be here otherwise. Is that why you were missing for a couple of weeks? Did you find a different muse?" she teased.

"Is this what we are going to do?" Karina's patience was running out. "Talk?"

"Well, maybe you should shut me up somehow." Raven smiled and kissed Karina's neck. She run her tongue all the way down to her breast, with one swift move she ripped Karina's blouse open. She turned her around and lowered down her jeans. Karina was no longer in control.

The brunette spread Karina's legs, she grabbed her hair with one hand and slipped the other inside her. She knew exactly what Karina wants and she was happy to give it to her. She pressed her body against Karina and sunk her teeth into Karina's neck, her finger went deeper and deeper inside her.

Karina's breath became much faster. She put one hand in Raven's hair and the other on her clit. She bend over a little more and pleasured herself. She came hard, harder than over the last few weeks and she needed it. All she wanted is for someone to know what to do to her.

For someone to take control and not treat her like a precious little princess. She needed to feel dominated as much as she liked to dominate. Her body fell lifeless on the sofa. Raven sat on top of her.

"Missed me," she smiled and kissed Karina.

"I fucking did," Karina answered. She pulled Raven up towards her face and let her move in the rhythm of the music as she pleasured her with her tongue. She kept her eyes open and put her hands on her breasts. She watched Raven as she came.

They stayed there for a while after. Talking and laughing, they finished the bottle and kissed good night.

"Thank you," said Karina as she put her leather jacket on and zipped it up to cover the broken buttons of her blouse.

"Anytime, honey," Raven smiled. "You know you can just call and I will come over. You don't have to come here."

"I like it here," Karina replied as she walked out of the room.

Alex

Alex woke up to the sound of birds outside the window; she must have forgotten to close it last night. She got up and opened the blinds. It was her second night in the apartment, but she didn't have a chance to see the view it offered just yet. A large, spread across the whole bedroom window was opening on a view of the city and the river she loved so much.

It was so peaceful and calm at this time of the day, the smell of the morning breeze hit her harder as she went out on the balcony. The sky was still mostly grey with sun trying to break through, successful in some parts more than others. The cranes in the background were starting to move slowly, like giants woken up from their peaceful sleep.

Alex noticed a tiny rainbow in the horizon. The most beautiful, colourful rainbow she has ever seen.

"If that's not a sign I don't know what is," Alex said out loud with a big smile on her face. For the first time in a long time, she was at peace, she was happy.

Knock on the door broke the silence lingering in the air. Alex threw on a T-shirt and a pair of boxers.

"Good morning, sunshine," said Noelle as soon as Alex opened the door. She was holding 2 coffees and a bag of croissants in her hand.

"What are you doing here?" Alex was both excited and surprised to see her.

"I came for breakfast," Noelle said playfully looking Alex up and down.

"Breakfast ha," Alex smiled as she gave Noelle a big hug. They stayed like that for a while, closeness gave them both a feeling of safety and peace they haven't known before.

"The coffee is getting cold." Noelle broke the silence again.

"Of course, come in," they walked into the bedroom and sat on the bed.

"Isn't it beautiful," Alex pointed at the window?

"Yes, it's quite something. I still can't believe you managed to get an apartment so close to the office."

"See I was always lucky, and I always get what I want." Alex had that cheeky, irresistible smile on her face. She put down her coffee on the bed side table and moved towards Noelle. She put her hand on Noelle's thigh.

"What about that breakfast?" She asked seductively.

"Here," Noelle pointed at the bag of croissants. She stood up and walked towards the door. "Want to give me a tour of the place?" She asked. Alex wasn't sure what was going on.

Noelle seemed a little distant but maybe she was in a rush for work. Alex took a day off to settle in her new place and to just take a breather. She felt she needed it after the last few weeks.

"Is everything OK?" Alex asked as she followed Noelle out of the bedroom.

"Yes, of course," Noelle answered with a confused look on her face. "Why do you ask?"

"No reason." Alex was trying to brush it off. She walked towards Noelle and was trying to kiss her. Noelle seemed distracted.

"Hey." Alex put her arms around Noelle. "It's OK." She looked into her eyes. "It's going to be OK." It seemed like that's what Noelle needed. She smiled and put her head on Alex's arm. She was breathing calmly, her eyes closed, as if she was trying to recharge her battery. She would love to keep this feeling everywhere she goes, this peace, this courage, this internal safety she felt around Alex. She couldn't however hold on to it when she was home. It took so much out of here to be two different people; she wished she knew how to merge the two.

"Thank you," she finally whispered. "It's been," she was trying to look for the right choice of words. "Confusing," she smiled.

"I can only imagine." Alex was so warm and patient. Non-judgmental and she didn't expect anything, it was refreshing. "Just give yourself time to process." She kissed Noelle's forehead.

"Just give yourself time to make any decisions. I don't want you to regret anything." Alex's patients nearly made it harder for Noelle. This lack of pressure meant all the choices were down to Noelle. Somehow it made it tougher.

"You're amazing." Noelle held on to Alex in a long hug. "You know that?" She continued. "You don't pressure me, you don't expect anything, you don't rush me. Why?"

"Oh, honey," Alex smiled. "I just know, deep down I know it's all going to work out and one day you will be able to wake up next to me. Every day."

Noelle closed her eyes once again and smiled. "I will talk to Liam soon, I promise. The boys' birthdays are coming up, then my birthday then Christmas. I just need some time to figure out when is the right time." She looked at Alex searching for understanding. "You know I want to."

"It's ok," Alex smiled. "You do what you must do when it's the right time. I'm not going anywhere. You know that." Noelle knew and that thought gave her comfort. Alex was hers and only hers even if she was the only one in the world who knew it.

"Hey," her energy went up a bit. "How about we go out on Friday after work?"

"Sure." Alex was happy to see the enthusiasm. "Where would you like to go?"

"I don't know," Noelle was once again excited. "Take me somewhere."

"I will do, Boss," Alex teased playfully. "Now come here and kiss me," she pulled Noelle closer. They kissed for a while, it seemed Noelle only now felt at ease. It took her a long time this morning to relax and give into the situation she was in.

The two parts of her were fighting some battle inside her, a battle no one outside of her knew bout. They finished the coffee and croissants and Noelle left for the office, leaving Alex craving for more.

Noelle

Morning coffee get togethers became her morning routine and she was looking forward to it each and every day. It gave her fuel for the day and some needed motivation to face her home life after work, during her time at home she always had Pinterest which created a subtle line of communication, it brought some excitement to her life.

She wanted to make changes, she wanted them soon; at the same time she didn't know how she can do this to Liam, not to mention the kids.

Over the years, she often had to stay at work late or meet business partners for an after-work dinner which turned into late night drinks. She didn't need to look for excuses or ask for permission, she just told Liam she won't be back till late. Which made things a little easier, it didn't however take any of the guilt away.

But that's something she didn't want to worry about, not today. Alex ended up taking the day off to catch up on some things and collect her remaining's from her old home, so they were meeting in town. Bite to eat and then few drinks. Alex was picking the location and Noelle was really looking forward to those few hours during which she can relax, enjoy her time, and forget about her reality about any sort of real-world problems.

Not that she had any. Her only problem was to pick one loving partner or another. Her settled, society approved life or a slightly more adventurous and riskier alternative. The latter was making her excited and made her feel alive, while the settled routine brought her a sense of security. She was torn between the two, but dint want to lose Alex.

She would do whatever she could to keep their love. She finished work and got ready in the bathroom in the office, she took a cab this morning as she didn't want to leave the car here over the weekend. She came out of the office around 6:30 and got into a taxi. She pulled on Capel Street outside a nice, charming pub on the corner. Alex was waiting outside.

"Hi, sexy." She greeted Alex with a big smile on her face.

"Well, hello, stranger." Alex let Noelle in front of her and they entered the pub.

Alex reserved a table at the back away from the window. They had a bit of privacy; Noelle appreciated the effort she could really relax and let her hair down. She was free to be herself. Same as the last time they drank, laughed, talked to strangers, danced, and kissed eagerly, kissed as if it was the last time, they were able to. Around 11, Noelle asked Alex.

"Can we go to yours?"

"Are you sure?" Alex asked looking at the time. She didn't know what time Noelle is planning on getting back, she didn't want her to do anything she will later regret.

"Maybe you're right, it's late." Noelle got a dose of reality. "Maybe next week?"

"That sounds like a plan."

They got out of the pub and got into two taxis. Alex went back to her apartment and Noelle went back home. Everyone was asleep by the time she came in. She went to the bathroom, took of her make up and went to the spare bedroom.

She didn't want to wake Liam and didn't want to sleep next to him, not tonight. Tonight, she wanted to imagine Alex. She wanted to remember how it felt being in Alex's arms till the morning. She fell asleep as soon as her head hit the pillow.

Alex got back to her apartment and stayed on her phone. She waited for a text that never came, she knew Noelle won't be able to text or pin or call once she gets home. She was still hoping she will make some effort to let her know she's OK. That she got home OK.

She knew she probably won't hear from her till Monday morning when they meet for a coffee. She got into empty bed and looked up on the black sky. This is how her heart felt tonight, every night. It was dark, distant and heavy. It felt like this every time she was away from Noelle and there was nothing she could do to change that.

Ironically, the only thing she could do was nothing. She had to be patient and trust that Noelle will get strength and be brave enough to make changes and give them a chance for a future together. A future that could be so amazing. This was the side reward for her decision.

The main and already visible changes were taking place in her life every day. She took control of her life, she was at ease, so peaceful and content with everything. No more fights, no more excuses, no more working on herself trying to please someone else.

She also didn't quite understand why she stayed in her previous relationship for so long. Things only became clear now once she had some distance and perspective. The issues, they started quite early; the feeling or rather lack of fulfilment both physical and emotional. She didn't want to look at it that way however.

She knew no amount of guilt can change the past and no amount of overthinking can influence the future. She wanted to be grateful for her time with Niamh, for whatever it brought into her life. She thought everyone came into her life for a reason and even if that reason might not be clear to her now at the time she needed it and it served a purpose.

She hoped Niamh was OK and that she thought of their past together in a similar way. She knew, however, her ex has some amount of healing and forgiveness to go through and it was not her journey. Not anymore. Now she had to focus on her own life, put aside the demons from the past and enjoy her present.

It was hard in the moment like this one. Lying there, in an empty bed with her heart and body longing for the person she loved. She imagined Noelle at home, is she with him? Do they lie in the same bed. Does he put his hands around her?

Alex didn't want her mind to go there; she didn't want to torment herself she pretended Noelle was home on her own, just with her two boys, with the twins. Alex looked forward to meeting them some day. They are a part of Noelle and they will be a part of her life. That however is something for another day.

Alex turned her attention from the sky and the moon to the empty pillow next to her. A tear appeared in a corner of her eye. She didn't want to give in. She closed her eyes and fell asleep.

Gabriela

The flight date was approaching fast. Gabriela had two weeks left in Ireland before she embarks on a journey to Italy; she wasn't sure how quick she will come back. The whole process could take anything from 3 to 9 months she was informed by her lawyer in Italy and she was glad she won't be here for a while. She didn't want to as everything remined her of her brief time with Karina.

It was silly and she knew however, head is one thing but the heart is another. She came into work that Sunday morning. She couldn't wait for her break as she just started a new book and she wanted to go back to it as soon as she could. Lose herself in this new story. Every story was a new adventure and the characters became her friends, she liked it more than TV or Netflix.

She was ready to head out for her 30 minutes escape from reality when she noticed Alex coming into the shop. She felt embarrassed but didn't want to be childish.

"Hi," she greeted Alex with a smile.

"Oh Hi." Alex was happy to see her in a better form. "I see you are doing much better."

"I am," she smiled. "Thank you and I'm sorry."

"It's absolutely fine." Alex was kind, she had kind eyes and a kind heart and she passed no judgement, she made everyone around her feel comfortable.

"Are you passing by or sitting in?" Gabriela asked. "I'm just about to go on my break if you would like some company? Unless your friend is coming by?"

"No, it's just me today," Alex smiled, "and yes that would be nice."

She took her coffee and went upstairs, taking a deep breath on the step where her and Noelle normally exchange their morning kiss. Away from everyone, away from anyone's eyes. She sat in their usual spot and waited for Gabriela who came up with her own coffee few minutes later.

"How are you?" Alex asked. "But I mean how are you really?" Gabriela knew what she meant.

"I'm OK, thank you for asking. That day outside your apartment. It was fresh, it just happened."

"Well, I'm glad to see you are fine, you do seem much better." Alex took a sip of her coffee.

"I'm going away to Italy for a couple of months soon so that's a good break form here and a fresh start," she added.

"That's awesome," Alex seemed genuinely happy for her.

"How are you?" Gabriela asked. "I don't want to overstep or make you feel uncomfortable. You and your friend." She blushed just asking the question or making an observation. "You two seem really happy and I would like to have that one day."

"It's complicated," Alex replied. She didn't want to say too much, she felt as if she was breaking confidence or betraying Noelle just talking about something what was their secret and their only. Gabriela, however, have seen them so she didn't think it was any harm to share. At the end of the day, it was her story too. "Not everything is what it seems." Alex added diplomatically.

"I see." Gabriela was now turning into a psychoanalyst she couldn't help it. "And how does that make you feel?" She asked. Alex laughed. She knew Gabriela is a therapist from their conversation in her apartment; she just didn't think she will try to do it to her.

"Don't analyse me," she continued laughing.

"I'm sorry," Gabriela blushed. "I can't quite help myself sometimes. This is juicy." They both smiled.

"It is." Alex wasn't going to say anymore.

"Are you OK?" Gabriela insisted, it was sweet her worry or rather concern for Alex.

"I am fine, I know what I'm doing. I know it's a 50/50 shot and I'm willing to try. I would always made that same choice."

"I know exactly what you mean," Gabriela lifted up her cup. "Here is to complicated, slightly dangerous and beautiful women." The comment brought an outburst of laughter from both of them.

"You sure are good." Alex made a remark. "Here is to all that, miss Gabriela, the therapist."

"That's not my professional opinion talking," she took a slight pause. "It's my experience as a lesbian in Dublin." She laughed again delighted with her funny comment.

"Either way you are on to something here."

Alex for a second felt as if she went to a therapy session. Gabriela's time was up an she had to go back to finish her shift. Alex did feel better after their chat. It's funny how one thing can led to another and under those weird circumstances they both have made a new friend.

If nothing else comes from this situation at least she has fer freedom and a friend. Not bad in comparison to few months ago. She finished her coffee and was about to leave when her phone lit up. Noelle rang her.

"Hey, I hope I'm not interrupting."

"Not at all." Alex was happy to hear from her.

"I'm sorry I couldn't reach you yesterday. Thank you so much for Friday. I had so much fun."

"Me too."

"Hey, I'm in the park with the boys." Noelle took a pause before she continued. "We are at a playground and probably will be here for another while. Would you like to come? And meet them."

"How is that going to work?" Alex was hoping this day will come. She was, however, afraid they were moving too fast.

"It's OK. There is plenty of moms here with their kids. Just come in and stand next to me, we can chat." The pause on the other line made Noelle nervous. "I would really like to see you, Alex, and this is the only way I can."

"OK," Alex answered. "I'll be down asap."

Alex

Against her better judgement, Alex jumped in the car and raced across town. The traffic was light so she made it to the park in 15 minutes. She didn't want to call Noelle, just in case something happened or she was back home at this point. She saw her car in the parking lot and it put a smile on Alex's face.

She rushed towards the playground and saw Noelle looking as perfect as ever, wearing a tight Nike tracksuit with her hair down. She walked through the gate to the playground hoping no one will question her in regards to not having a child.

"Hey." She approached Noelle slowly not knowing if this is OK.

"Hi," Noelle replied eagerly. "I am so happy to see you."

"Me too." Alex didn't want to get too close. She didn't want to raise the boys suspicion. It took all her strength not to hug or kiss Noelle. "Where are they?"

"Over there," Noelle pointed at two tall for their age, identical twins. They had Noelle's face and blue eyes. They were playfully running around the slide.

"They are gorgeous," Alex was watching them curiously. The boys lost interest and came down to their mom to get a drink.

"I want ice cream," said the first one.

"No, I want McDonalds," said the other.

"Ice cream first" "no McDonalds" "Ice cream"—the argument between them seemed to go on for a while.

"It's better to leave them to it," Noelle laughed looking at Alex who wasn't sure if it's OK to talk or interact. She wasn't sure what she can or cannot do. She had to just trusted her intuition.

"You know you can get ice cream at McDonalds," she said delighted with her adulting.

"Can you take us?" One of the twins responded.

"Yes, can you take us?" The other followed his brother as if they knew her for ages.

"The lady has to stay here with her own kids," Noelle corrected them. "She can't take you what would her kids think," she continued.

"Where are your kids?"

"Yes, can we play with them?" Alex started to break a sweat around her forehead. What the hell am I going to tell them, she thought.

"How about you two go play for 10 more minutes before we go to McDonalds and get that ice cream." They both gave Alex a curious look and smiled on their way back to the play area.

"Bye, bye," the both shouted at the same time.

"I'm so sorry," Noelle looked at Alex. "I probably shouldn't drag you here."

"It's OK," Alex smiled. She wanted so badly to at least touch Noelle and comfort her. "This was nice. They are great," she was genuinely taken back by them both. They were a part of Noelle and she felt she could love them as much as she loves their mom. "You are great with them," Alex added.

"Thank you," Noelle smiled. "And thank you so much for coming even for a few minutes it means a lot."

"Of course."

They talked for a couple of minutes. Alex left first not wanting to raise any more suspicious leaving the playground by herself. She got into the car with a smile on her face and a warmth around her heart. This was nice and different at the same time.

Could this be her every day soon? She wasn't sure before but now she knew. One look at the boys, seeing their mom in their little faces. It melted her heart.

Noelle

Noelle and the boys arrived home a while later. Trips to McDonalds are always fun with two hyper 8 year olds. This time, however, nothing bothered her. She had a smile on her face, an unusual smile. As she pulled in the drive way Liam went out of the house to greet them.

"You look happy."

"I guess I am," Noelle replied. She didn't want Liam to question her or notice anything different.

"All good," he looked at the boys. "Oh, McDonalds I see. I guess daddy doesn't have to make dinner tonight." He opened the door and helped Noelle out, kissed her on the cheek. She froze slightly. "You OK?" he asked noticing her shiver.

"Yes, I'm fine. They were great," she pointed at the kids trying to deflect from his question. "Even in McDonalds they didn't behave like little savages." Liam laughed.

"Mommy made a friend," one of the lads shouted out.

"A friend? Nice." Liam didn't make anything of it. Noelle's heart, however, stopped.

"Yes," the other guy continued. "Mommy made a nice friend, she was a pretty lady."

Liam looked at Noelle.

"Yes, Mommy gave a wrong example," she laughed nervously. "I chatted to a stranger in the playground as the boys were playing. Some other mom." Liam didn't make anything of it, he normally always talked to other parents.

"She's not a stranger," one of the boys blurred out. "I saw her before."

Noelle's body turned stone cold. She could feel her blood turn into ice and cold sweat run down her neck. She didn't know how was this possible. How can the boys have seen her?

Was it a picture, was it an IM on her phone? Pinterest? Did they see them in town one of the evenings? She thought she was careful. She couldn't say anything she felt paralysed.

"And where did you see her?" Liam laughed.

"In my dreams," the boy shouted as he run into the house.

"Their imagination is something else," Liam laughed. "Are you OK?" Liam looked at Noelle. "You look as if you saw a ghost."

"I'm OK. I think got up too quick."

"Oh you have to watch that now." Liam put out his hand to help her find her balance. "Hopefully, your vertigo isn't coming back. How about you take a bath and relax and I will get the boys settled for bed."

"I will, thank you," Noelle replied in what sounded like a whisper.

Liam kissed her cheek and went inside. Leaving her outside to catch her breath. She couldn't believe what just happened. She couldn't believe her selfish act back fired so quickly. She felt guilty for putting the boys in that situation.

She couldn't, however, go another day without seeing Alex, without looking into her brown eyes, without hearing her voice. She felt as if she was losing her mind. She didn't want Liam to know, not like this, not ever. She had to be more careful, not take risks.

She laughed at the end thinking about how she questioned everything; started tracing back everything she did over the last few weeks just because of a little comment from an 8 year old. She calmed down after a while, made a glass of camomile tea and indeed run a bath. She locked the bathroom and got in.

She took a picture of her legs and send it to Alex. The situation from earlier seemed to add to the excitement. She send a picture with a caption.

'Wish you were here.'

She knew Alex won't reply. They set boundaries and she won't break them. She was the only one allowed to break the rules.

Karina

The plane landed in Athens; Karina was excited to get away again. She loved her work, she loved getting out and about and taking pictures. Capturing unforgettable moments and meeting people. It was the best part of what she was doing.

Sometimes, she would go by herself and create the most imaginative and amazing collections. Sometimes she freelanced and took contracts and worked for different companies, magazines, papers, or media adds. The opportunities always brought a lot of freedom which she also enjoyed.

This time she had a couple of weeks in Greece. She took a contract for few sessions, after that she was going to go to Italy. One of the galleries wanted to display some of her work, her contract was already negotiated; she had to set up the scene and agree on the details, amount of prints and so on. She was excited and couldn't wait to see the space.

In the meantime, her own gallery in Dublin was getting a couple of collections from around the world which was a huge success and something she worked on for the last few months. It was all coming together, this year has proven to be the best one yet. She got to her hotel. A girl at the reception reminded her of Gabriela and she couldn't help but feel bad for how things went.

For how quickly and abruptly she changed towards her. Karina knew it didn't happen just that morning; she was growing tired of someone coming across so needy, she wanted strength not someone who would bend their will for her pleasure. She should, however, be honest with Gabriela and not let her walk into a sort of a trap.

Things escalated that morning and Karina knew she had enough. She should, however, have stopped it few weeks earlier, not play with the girls feelings. And for that she felt a little guilty. She knew she will be in Italy in a couple of weeks and if she's lucky, Gabriela might be in the same city.

If she happens to be in Milan at the same time they can meet for dinner, she would like to apologise, in person not over a call or text. She knew nothing will ever come from this short affair she felt however she owns her that much.

"Hey, I will be in Milan in about three to four weeks. Let me know where you are and maybe we can grab dinner. I feel I wasn't honest with you. I owe you an explanation."

She texted Gabriela straight away; she liked to get things off her list. She was not one to procrastinate. She sat at the desk and opened her laptop. Scrolled through emails and checked if everything was set up for the next few weeks. All seemed in order.

She ordered room service and decided to have a glass of wine before it arrives. She thought of the other night with Raven; an idea went through her head to invite her over, to spend a couple of days here. She knew, however, this will be a distraction and she didn't want any distractions, not while she works.

Going to the club was more of a leisure and she didn't want to bring that into her work. No, her work was pure and innocent, superb not perversive and seductive. She didn't know how she feels about going back there. She liked Raven, she felt satisfied by her however she wanted something more.

She knew something inside her is changing. Maybe it's the age, maybe it's the travelling, maybe it's the money. She wanted someone she can share it with and someone she feels safe with. That person was yet to be born. Knock on the door broke her day dream. Maybe for the best.

Alex

The sound of a popping champagne bottle caught Alex's attention. She looked up from the screen. Noelle and most of the office were celebrating in the meeting room. She smiled as she send out the email. She knew this was coming.

They broke a deal with the eastern-European markets. Mostly thanks to Alex's ides and hard work. Five new countries were added to the distribution list. For now smaller branches but who knows how this will spread. Alex was both proud of her work and intuition and happy for Noelle and her company.

She felt like she had so much to contribute for both the company and its boss. She felt accomplished. Somehow she always had this feeling inside her that she has to do more, she has to prove her worth to Noelle and with this deal she has done that. She sent an email and was now able to join the celebration.

Someone handed her a glass of champagne as she entered the meeting room. Few toasts and a couple of speeches later she was back in her office with Noelle sitting on the corner of her desk. Everyone knew they have to discuss details so for once they were able to just talk openly, without hiding.

"Well done," Noelle was trying to keep it professional. "That's some great work, Alex."

"Thank you." Alex played the game. "So what now?" she asked.

"Now we go to Poland," Noelle smiled. She had that idea in her head for a while and she knew once the deal goes ahead it will be their excuse to get away. "So, I pulled some strings here and there, and organised our main eastern office to be opened in your home town." Noelle smiled she could see both surprise and delight on Alex's face.

"Considering someone has to make sure all goes well, a trip to set everything up is in order," she continued with a big delighted smile on her face. "Obviously the CEO has to go herself and considering it is your deal, well, you will have to go also."

"And when is that business trip planned for?" Alex could hardly contain her excitement. Not for travelling to her home town nor the deal itself but the promise of having Noelle for a week to herself. The freedom, the experience, the adventure they are going to have was filling Alex's head with so many ideas.

"Next month, we need to set things up, so let's say three or four weeks."

"That sounds reasonable," Alex was trying to stay professional, she tried to remind herself they are in the office. "I will make any necessary arrangements."

"We should celebrate tonight," Noelle lowered her voice. "Not with drinks or office party but you know," she played with her hair before she whispered, "you and me."

"That could be arranged." Alex was happy with today's news and the prospect of spending some time with Noelle. She never knows when a chance like this will present itself.

"Where would you like to go?" Alex asked.

"I'm thinking we take your car and head to yours after work?"

"I like that." That put Alex in an even better mood, she didn't have to share Noelle with anyone else today.

Alex was counting down the hours till they can leave. Noelle let everyone go home a bit earlier today, after the office celebration. A couple of people, however, stubbornly stayed till the normal 'closing' time. It was approaching 6 pm, Alex and Noelle met by the elevator.

"I should fire everyone who didn't leave today," Noelle laughed.

"You really should," that amused Alex, sometimes she forgot Noelle had all this power. She didn't flaunt it nor she ever used it. "I'm glad you decided to come to mine today."

"Yea," Noelle was in a playful mood. "How so?"

"Well," Alex smiled. "No reason really."

They were chatting as they got into the car, Alex enjoyed driving Noelle. This felt so normal, so easy and as if it was meant to be. She hoped one day it will be their reality. Alex pulled into the car park and they both rushed towards the elevator.

"Tell me about the trip." Alex still couldn't believe it was actually happening.

"Well, I just want you all for myself." Noelle put her head on Alex's arm as they stood in the elevator. "I think this will be a nice start to, you know," she looked at Alex. "Our future."

"Oh yea." Alex let Noelle get out of the elevator as she looked for her keys. She opened the apartment door. "And how is that future going to look like?" She was curious what Noelle has in mind.

"I don't know, maybe we live here, maybe we get a bigger place. We will need some extra bedrooms for the boys." Noelle walked into the apartment, put her bag and jacket on the chair. "I think after we come back, it will be a good time to talk to Liam," she continued casually.

"And then we just live together?" Alex felt Noelle skipped a couple of steps but she was happy to go with this vision.

"Well, sure in a couple of months." Noelle made herself at home as she sat on the coach. "Somewhere down the line we will get married also." At this point, Alex felt this was a way too casual approach to the conversation. As much as she enjoyed all of the promises Noelle was making.

"And you were going to inform me of all this when exactly?" She laughed.

"Oh, don't worry. I will give you enough notice. Now come here." Noelle pointed a spot next to her on the coach. Alex wanted to have a sort of normal, relaxing evening.

"Should we order some food?" Alex asked turning on the TV. Noelle took the remote from her hand.

"I have all the food I need right here." She turned the TV off and bit Alex's lip.

"I see," Alex insisted on having a girlfriend like experience with Noelle. "Would you like to watch a movie?" She asked. Noelle seemed to be running out of patience.

"I can watch a movie at home," she replied sharply. Alex looked at Noelle in disbelief, she was surprised by her reaction. She has never seen her like this. "I'm sorry." Noelle felt bad.

"I just don't get a chance to see you as often as I would like, to be with you, to touch you whenever I want. I just want this to be perfect."

"I understand." Alex liked the softer version of Noelle. "Come here," she gave her a hug and kissed her lips. "I am right here." Noelle smiled, she was calmer now and went back to talking about their time together.

"So, what are you going to show me in Poland?" She asked curiously.

"Well, we will definitely spend a lot of time in the hotel room, except for when we have to work of course. I will bring you to my mom's for dinner. You can meet my friends and some of my family." Noelle felt a bit shook. It all sounded great but meeting family however, felt like a sort of a serious step.

"That would be nice," she replied. "I would love that actually." She felt close to Alex, closer than ever before. Planning this trip has made them both excited, happy and hopeful for the future.

The evening was getting darker and Noelle didn't want to waste any more time. She started kissing Alex and shortly after they moved to the bedroom. They spend hours just talking, kissing, enjoying each other's bodies.

She knew with the new deal she will spend more time in the office, planning and celebrating. That meant more time with Alex. It got late pretty quick and Noelle had to go back home. They ordered a taxi. Alex hoped with all of her heart that this will change soon.

She never wanted to expect anything, she didn't want to put any presser on either Noelle or this relationship. Noelle, however, changed the rules of the game. She planted a seed in Alex's mind and her heart, and Alex hoped this will grow and come to fruition soon.

Gabriela

The plane landed; Gabriela felt both relief and anticipation as to what will come next. She booked an appointment with a local barber she felt this new start deserves a change. She always wanted to try a different, short haircut and she felt adventurous enough to go for what she wanted.

Being in a place where no one knows you brought a different sense of comfort. She could be herself in Dublin but here she could really relax and just do whatever felt right. She packed a lot of books, she knew this will take time she might even start learning Italian.

With all this free time on her hands the possibilities were endless. She might even be able to mend her broken heart. After a few minutes, her phone connected to a local network and she was able to check what she missed out on during her two-hour flight. A couple of emails, a missed call from her friend and a text.

She couldn't believe when the name flashed up on her screen. She opened it, she could feel her heart jumping in her chest.

"Hey, I will be in Milan in about 3 to 4 weeks. Let me know where you are and maybe we can grab dinner. I feel I wasn't honest with you. I owe you an explanation."

She smiled; that's fair, she thought. She knew she deserved some sort of explanation as to what happened that morning. What changed. She knew this will only be a short meeting and she didn't have any illusion that something could ever grow from this relationship.

They were too different, they belonged to two different worlds she was however, happy Karina reached out as it was a promise for closure. A closure she needed. She didn't expect any communication and this was a nice surprise. She looked up and realised the plane is nearly empty.

She grabbed her bag from the overhead storage and went towards the exit smiling. She collected her luggage which took way too long and got a taxi to her new place, her new home for the next few months. She rented a small one bed flat away from the city, an option which was the cheapest and sort of nice. The apartment had a kitchen and small living room, the bedroom overlooked an old street with cobble stones.

The apartment was an attic apartment with slanty ceilings. It was cute and cosy and most of all just hers. She didn't have to share an apartment or a room which was a nice change. She didn't mind the size she just loved an idea of having her own space for the next few months. Her little piece of heaven.

She left the bags in the bedroom and put on a kettle. She grew fond of tea with milk, the Irish way. It brought a bit comfort. A comfort she needed right now. She knew she has few long months ahead of her. She took out her phone and looked at the text once again.

The thought of being able to see a familiar face soon made her happy, especially Karina's face. I will need to reply, she thought as she poured hot water into the cup. What should I say, she wondered. It needs to be something casual but nice. She didn't want to come across rude nor overly excited. She didn't want to spook Karina or make it look like she was too eager.

"Hey," she started typing. "I'm not far from Milan." What a happy coincidence, she thought. "You don't owe me anything." That felt mature. "But it will be nice to see you." She kept it light and short.

She put her phone away, sat in front of the window with a fresh cup of tea and enjoyed both the view and the peace around her.

Karina

Her days were busy, which is exactly what she liked while working. She travelled from one location to the next with a whole tribe of models, make-up artists, directors and a couple of back up photographers. They mostly took pictures of the surrounding areas and prepped the set. She, however, had the vision and skill to make this magical, extraordinary.

It was her first contract of this type and it was an exciting experience. A new journey, new adventure. She needed something different to break her routine and provide a source of inspiration.

Her time in Greece was now coming to an end, a bittersweet feeling. Karina grew fond of the beautiful views around her hotel, she always loved nature and there was plenty of it around. The warm weather, beautiful wine, and food. She will miss it when she's back in Dublin, before that happens however, she had another stop to make. A stop she already felt excited about. She hasn't been in Italy in a while and had a few friends to catch up with, that and the coffee.

She will stock up on the coffee before travelling home. It used to amuse her seeing all these people stopping in café's all over the place just to indulge in that tiny size espressos. At first, she didn't get it, growing up and living in America most of her life where everything is super-sized it seemed like a complete opposite. Now however she couldn't think of anything worse than picking up half a litre coffee on your way to the office.

It seemed unsophisticated, barbarian even. She much preferred a quick espresso in an Italian café, some were small some a little bigger but all full of character, and those beautiful pastries. She didn't realise how much she missed it till now. She was looking forward to her next trip even more.

Gabriela

It was a sunny and beautiful day in Milan. The streets were full of people, elderly couples walking around, teenagers chatting, kids laughing, a couple of tourists drinking coffee at the side of the street outside many bars and cafe's. Gabriela was curious about how the conversation is going to go and what Karina has to say, she wasn't exited or scared. Not like in the past.

The couple of weeks in Italy have given her time to think, time to refocus and reconnect with herself. She met her solicitor nearly every week and filled a never ending amount of papers in order to secure her Italian citizenship and passport before she can return to Dublin as an European citizen. It will bring so many new possibilities and she will finally be able to start working in her field. Or whatever was close to it anyway.

Dinner seemed a bit too formal so she asked Karina to meet up for a coffee instead. Karina picked a little café at a corner of two charming streets in Milan. Gabriela took a bus that morning. She was staying 30 minutes from the city which gave her both an easy access and peace.

She arrived early but she was happy to have some time to take in the scenery. She walked into the café and picked a table with a bench on each side. That will give Karina an option to either sit next to her or opposite to her which will give them both a bit of comfort and it will give her a feeling of safety.

She didn't want to be too close to her, even though she didn't see her for months; she was afraid one look might bring the old feelings back. She didn't want to put herself in too close proximity. She ordered a black coffee and took in the surroundings.

Dimmed lights complemented the leather brown couches and wooden floors. The walls were purple and covered with pictures, old Italian men, fruit market, coffee beans, old sculptures and a beautiful pizzeria. She noticed a picture of a young girl in white dress, sitting on a fence. The picture was black and white and all the colours were quite dark, except for the dress.

The girl had black hair and a beautiful angelic face. It can't be, Gabriela thought. Why was she so drawn to this picture, she looked at the right bottom corner at the photographers initials.

KF'

Of course it's you, she laughed out loud. You touch people everywhere you go even if you are not there. She looked around the café and most of the pictures had the same initial. No wonder she picked this place. All of the sudden, Gabriela felt as if Karina was watching her from each and every picture, through each and every eye.

She could feel her presence from every frame. At that moment, a subtle sound of a bell broke her train of thought. Karina walked into the café. Dressed in cream pants and matching suit jacket, her hair was curly and a little messy, her almond eyes just as Gabriela remembered.

"I like your hair," Karina greeted her. "It's so short," she touched the side of her face. "It suits you," she smiled and sat across from Gabriela which brought a sense of relief.

"Hi to you too." Gabriela was trying to keep it cool.

"Hi," Karina smiled. "Black coffee please, house beans of course, thank you." She ordered her coffee in Italian; the barista seemed to appear as soon as she walked in.

"Didn't know you speak Italian," Gabriela made an observation. It seemed she didn't know Karina at all. She was finding it hard to recognise her. She seemed different, maybe it was her, maybe it was Karina or maybe it was the Italian air.

"I also speak Persian, Spanish, English, Italian and a bit of Arabic. I'm conversational anyway." She didn't have to say anything to impress Gabriela but she couldn't help herself. "So how are you? Anything exciting happening except the hair cut?" She smiled trying her best to lighten the mood.

"You tell me," Gabriela tried to turn the tables, she pointed at the pictures around them. "Have you left a piece of yourself everywhere in Italy or is it just here?"

"I didn't think you will notice." Karina laughed. "This is new actually, the owner is," she paused. "Well, an old friend of mine. She asked me to refresh the look. I took those just last week around town, do you like them?"

"Yes," Gabriela smiled. "Very much so," she continued. "They are, well, perfect just like you." She didn't mean to say that, she didn't want to say that.

"Well, thank you," Karina smiled but she pulled away leaning her back against the warm wooden frame of the bench.

"I didn't mean to make you feel uncomfortable." Gabriela could read her body language.

"No, it's OK." Karina moved closer towards the table. "I should have told you I will be all over the walls," she made a joke, it helped Gabriela relax.

"A little heads up would have been nice." Gabriela smiled.

She, however, understood now why nothing could ever happen between them, nothing serious anyway. Karina was a free spirit, a free soul, she was unattainable, she wasn't going to settle for anyone. She had 'old friends' in every city just like a sailor had a mistress in every port.

Gabriela felt a sense of closure she didn't think she will get from this meet up. She felt relieved and at ease. She understood the moment she got too comfortable in Karina's company, too familiar, Karina could no longer see her. It is not her style. Commitment, closeness, it's not something she wants and Gabriela had to honour that. She just wished she knew before hand, but she appreciated Karina at least tried.

"Listen," Karina broke the silence. "I'm sorry for the way things unravelled, for the way I treated you I should have been gentler. You didn't deserve what happened and I want you to know it's not you, you have done nothing wrong." Gabriela smiled, it was nice to hear those words even if she already knew that.

"Thank you, but you don't owe me anything, especially not an apology. You never hid who you are, you never lied or promised anything. You were always open and honest. I guess I thought I can change you." Gabriela laughed.

"I thought we will ride off into the sunset on your white stallion."

"If it's my stallion it would have been black," Karina made a joke.

"See, I can't even get the colour of the horse right." They both laughed, they understood each other.

"Maybe in the next life time?" Karina was now relaxed. She reminded Gabriela of when they first met, the leather sofa's around them, Karina's pictures in the frames all over the walls, even though Gabriela knew her to some extent Karina was still a mystery. A beautiful puzzle she will never be able to solve.

"Thank you for, well coming here, reaching out." Gabriela looked at the watch they were talking for nearly an hour.

"Of course, I mean it's the least I can do," as she spoke, a tall, brown haired, Italian woman came to the table. She spoke English with a strong Italian accent.

"I'll be ready in 10 minutes." She spoke to Karina as she kissed her cheek. "Is your friend joining us for dinner?" She looked at Gabriela.

"I don't think she is," Karina answered. "Would you like to?"

"No, thank you very much," Gabriela was caught off guard. "Enjoy, ladies. I have a couple of errands to run." They both knew it wasn't true, Gabriela didn't want to put herself in any other uncomfortable situation.

"That's a pity," the beautiful Italian stranger was looking her straight in the eyes. "She's delicious," she added as she walked away from the table.

"10 minutes," she repeated. Gabriela was not surprised. Nothing would surprise her when it came to Karina.

"An old friend ha?"

"What can I say." Karina didn't even seem slightly embarrassed or uncomfortable. She never apologised for who she was and she was so many things.

Karina and her Italian friend left the café a few minutes later. Gabriela ordered another coffee and a slice of cake and watched them walk before they disappeared around the corner. Like the sailor in his ship disappearing in the horizon.

Gabriela somehow knew this was the last time she will ever see Karina, even with that thought she was content. She closed a somewhat beautiful chapter in her life and it made her stronger, and for that she will always be grateful.

Noelle

The trip was coming up quicker than Noelle anticipated. Time seemed to go very fast and juggling her now double life was taking its toll. Noelle didn't want to lie or deceive, she didn't want to be two different people however, she didn't know how else was this possible. On one hand, the safety and security of her marriage, on the other the excitement of the relationship with Alex and finally allowing herself to be her.

To feel, to not be ashamed of her passion and desire, something she struggled with for so long. It seemed she buried her thoughts so deep, before she met Alex she forgot what it feels like to love, to desire, to feel satisfaction on both emotional and physical level. Alex has woken that inside her and the more she got the more she wanted.

As soon as she quenched her thirst however, a feeling of overwhelming guilt would take over. Guilt because of what's she was doing, because of lying and guilt for being with Alex. She was torn between her two realities and she knew she needs to make some changes before it consumes her. She was angry and found herself easily agitated; a feeling of rage came creeping in and her patience was getting shorter.

The smallest thing would throw her off and she knew she can't keep going this way. She wasn't overly careful either, she would go out with Alex and dance with her, kiss her. She would make sure the whole club knows they are together, as if she hoped someone will see her and she won't have to lie anymore.

She knew one day it will stop and deep down she was afraid how her life will change. She didn't know if she was ready for this. Will she ever be ready. She wanted to, she needed this change. She loved Alex and her heart, body and mind were craving her all the time they were not together. She knew her conversation with Liam is coming closer and closer.

"We are ready in the meeting room." Her PA's voice broke the silence.

"Thank you, Katy" Noelle replied. "I will be there in 5 minutes. Are the flights booked?"

"Yes," she replied. "Flights but not the accommodation, would you like me to make the arrangements."

"No, thank you. That won't be necessary." Noelle smiled, the PA left the office. She didn't want anyone to look after that part of the business trip as Alex was taking care of the arrangement. Besides, she didn't want the office to know they are booking one instead of two rooms.

Noelle walked into the meeting room where weekly briefing was about to start. She liked to give her employees independence, she let them run the meetings and she found it worked quite well as they always put in the extra work. They seemed to like the responsibility and trust.

Noelle caught Alex's eye and smiled. A shy, subtle smile and a secret that came with it, a secret only they knew about. For now anyway. Noelle didn't want it to be some dirty little office romance. She looked at Alex. Her strong arms, athletic build, perfect hair and beautiful eyes.

If she could she would just walk towards her, kiss her in front of everyone, she wanted everyone to know she is hers. She could see how both men and women looked at her and it made her proud and jealous at the same time. Jealous because they didn't need to pretend. They could just let their eyes say it all. The meeting ended and Noelle caught Alex's attention before she left the room.

"Could you come to my office in a few minutes please," she said with the most professionalism she could find within herself. "We need to discuss the details of the trip."

"Of course," Alex replied.

Alex

Alex waited for Noelle to get back into her office before she made her way in. She enjoyed the game their played, it was exciting, the subtle smiles, hungry looks. She hoped however it will soon stop. She didn't care if people know or not, she didn't want to talk to anyone about this, she wanted however to just be herself around Noelle inside and outside of work. She walked into Noelle's office trying to wipe a big smile of her face.

"You wanted to see me?" She enjoyed this part, as if their relationship was strictly professional. Noelle was the boss and most of the office probably fantasised about what they had at some point, they can have their fantasies however she had it all.

"Yes, Alex, please sit down." She looked at her PA. "Can you make sure they know of our arrival. I would like to look at a couple of offices and possibly have a few interviews. Can you make sure everything is arranged for two weeks from now."

"Of course." Katy smiled at Alex while taking Noelle's notes. "Anything else?" She asked.

"No, that would be all and please close the door." Katy nodded and left the office.

"Plenty to organise," Alex made an observation.

"You have no idea." Noelle was extremely busy with all the arrangements but the idea of the trip excited her. "You will be doing most of it."

"OK, Boss." Alex was showing her off dimples which always accompanied her cheeky smile.

"Do you have to be so cute?" Noelle wanted to jump across the desk, sit on her lap and just kiss her.

"I guess it's my default."

"I guess it is." Noelle smiled, she was soft around Alex. "So two weeks, I can't believe we will get on a plane and just be able to be together."

"Me neither, it seems surreal. I'm so happy its coming so quick. I really want to just have you for myself. Not having to share you."

"I know," Noelle had sadness in her eyes. "It will be amazing. For now, let's actually do what we are supposed to."

Alex moved her chair closer as the planning was taking a lot of their time. The actual work part. There was so much to organise, so many meetings, viewings for the office and some interviews for suitable staff. Noelle opened offices in other parts of Europe before but here she completely relied on Alex, something she wasn't used to but definitely enjoyed.

"I could get used to this." She looked at Alex with a smile on her face and dreamy eyes.

"This?" Alex wasn't sure what she meant.

"Yes, this." She touched Alex's leg under the table. She knew her desk is fully covered so no one will be able to see even if they stood outside the large glass door. She moved it higher to her thigh. "This, you sitting so close to me at work. Doing things in the past I had to handle by myself. It's nice to have someone I can rely on. Both personally and professionally."

Alex found it hard to focus with Noelle's hand still travelling up and down her inner thigh. "I would like it to stay this way, you know at work. Regardless of what might or might not happen outside of work."

This is the first time Noelle brought this subject up, at work and in general this is the first time she indicated things might not work out.

"You mean after we get married?" Alex made a joke. She felt like the mood needs lightening.

"Yea, that too," Noelle laughed.

"Of course," Alex squeezed Noelle's hand still residing on her thigh. "Whatever happens, happens, right? And whatever doesn't happen, we will deal with it and figure it out as we go." That gave Noelle a sense of peace, she felt safe with Alex, safe in the unknown and safe with what was going on between them.

"Your 3 pm is here," Katy's voice interrupted them. She opened the door slightly. Both Noelle and Alex jumped.

"Thank you, I'll be there in 5," Noelle was icy and sharp as if nothing was going on. Katy didn't seem to notice, Alex thought.

"Thank you, Alex, that will be all for now." She turned towards her lover as if the only thing between them was a strictly professional relationship. Alex stood up a little surprised how quickly Noelle could turn from one character to the next. How well can she play this game.

Has she done it before? Alex thought for the first time, but as soon as the thought came she chased it away. "Please let me know if you need anything else," said Alex as she walked towards the door. Katy was still there holding it slightly open. They walked out together.

"We need to organise an office party," Katy smiled to Alex. "You know before you guys travel. We need to celebrate such a success."

"Yes, that would be nice," Alex replied. The party will be something they need to attend and play a part in, the travel is what she really looked forward to.

"We can always do it when we are back," she added. "When we actually have something to celebrate."

"That's even a better idea. The next two weeks will be busy, it's better to leave it till after. I will mark something in the calendar and talk to Noelle."

"When are you going back?" Katy asked. "I will need to organise another flight and a hotel?"

"Going back where?" Alex wasn't sure what she meant.

"To Poland," Katy seemed surprised. "You are both going for a week right? Normally, someone goes back then for a couple of months to make sure all is working correctly. You know there is so much admin, contracts, deliveries, distribution all other things that need to be checked and set up."

"I thought with this being your big win it's you who will stay or go back and you can be with your family that would be nice."

"Yes, it would." Alex smiled trying not to look too surprised. "I didn't talk details with Noelle yet, that's the next part."

"Ah great." Katy seemed genuinely helpful. "Let me know if you need me to set anything up. Tickets, meetings anything," she added as she walked towards her desk.

"I will do. Thank you," Alex answered as politely as possible trying to not to show any signs of surprise . She wasn't sure if or when Noelle was going to tell her about the exact plans. Surely it was going to be her setting everything up but being away from Noelle for a couple of months didn't seem right.

She didn't think Noelle would be happy with that either. Unless that's why she didn't say anything. Maybe she wanted to send someone else.

Gabriela

The weeks flew by and Gabriela was getting fond of the Italian streets, their coffee and culture. She missed Dublin a little less and started to realise she will miss Italy. She made a trip to Milan her weekly ritual. It must have been just after lunch as the streets became quieter and the little cafes were not as busy.

She walked into her now favourite café and sat in the corner. The window was close so she could look into the street, it wasn't too close however, which allowed her to get lost in her book. She didn't come here in hope to see Karina, but it did give her comfort that a piece of someone who was once so close to her heart was right there, looking at her from every frame. She could feel her presence even after few weeks have passed.

"Your usual?" A female voice asked.

"Yes please," Gabriela smiled. Karina's 'old friend' owned the café. Adrianna was a tall, good looking Italian woman with a strong will and a soft heart. She was different than Karina yet in some ways similar. She brough the coffee to Gabriela's table and sat down next to her.

Gabriela smiled as this has never happened before. The place was empty so she had it all to herself, even the attention of the owner.

"So," Adrianna started a conversation. "What brings you here every week? You are not hoping to find Karina here one day?"

"No," Gabriela felt silly, is this what it looked like?

"Good," Adrianna laughed. "She is a free spirit you know."

"Oh, I know," Gabriela joined the laughter. "How do you know her? Are you two," she took a pause and looked for courage to ask that question.

"Lovers?" Adrianna was obviously more comfortable as she jumped in mid-sentence.

"No ," she continued. "We are good old friends, we go way back. That's all." For some reason Gabriela felt a sense of relief. It would make her feel weird if they both slept with or loved the same woman.

"How did you meet." She felt braver and more inquisitive. She wanted to know the story. Adrianna smiled as her eyes became absent for a second as if she was reaching for a past memory.

"It's a long story. You sure you have time?" Gabriela wasn't sure if she was joking or if she was serious.

"I have all the time in the world," she answered.

"Oh, OK then." Adrianna made herself comfortable and whistled at a waiter before she started the story. "I met Karina years ago. We were just kids really, maybe twenty." Her Italian accent was strong but she tried her best to speak fluent English. Throwing Italian words here and there.

"Karina wanted to be a photographer. She was a photographer, artist really but she wanted to be famous. Me, on the other hand, I always wanted to serve coffee. I grew up on a farm with my parents, and grew custom to good coffee beans. You know the smell and taste of fresh coffee in the morning?"

She looked at Gabriela but continued without waiting for her response.

"I mean a really fresh one, when you roast and grind the beans yourself not the shit you buy in a store. Well, my dream was to give people the best coffee they will ever have."

"Your coffee is good," Gabriela thought this needed a compliment. Adrianna threw a cold, sharp look and continued.

"I wanted to give people that same experience I had. That fresh taste anytime of the day. I met Karina in Spain on holidays. Her dad was Spanish so she wanted to see where she came from. We met and clicked straight away, we went on a date even and it was awful, she's too stubborn," Adrianna laughed.

"So anyway we knew we are going to be great friends, sometimes you just know. I came back home to Italy and she came with me to see the farm and the fields I have told her so much about. She fell in love with it just like I did. I told her about my dream and she told me about hers and we made a promise to help each other, always."

Adrianna smiled and took a sip of her perfectly brewed coffee before she continued. "Karina looked into the paper, every day for a month, one day she came to me and said. Look there is a coffee shop in Milan and it's for rent. It was cheap but we didn't have any other details. It didn't stop us. We got into my parents car, took few bags of coffee beans and embarked on a journey to Milan to meet the owner; a journey that changes out life's forever. Karina took pictures on the way, fields, forest, towns anything she found fascinating. We got to Milan, the café was away from town, on the outskirts." She took another sip and continued.

"It didn't matter it was perfect. It was tiny we could barely fit in 3 tables inside but it had a window which made it easy to sell to people passing on the street. We opened up within two weeks doing all the repairs ourselves. Karina even spend the last of her money to get frames for some pictures she took on the way. We put the pictures up and on the day of opening she brought a record player and some jazz records. No one around played Jazz. I thought it was crazy but apparently it was not. It brought a lot of customers. Karina helped every day and even though we didn't make a lot of money it was enough to keep us both going, we didn't have to go back to our homes."

"That's an amazing story." Gabriela felt touched that Adrianna would share this with her.

"Do I look like I'm finished." She took another sip of her coffee. One day a man came in, very well dressed. Karina knew he owned a gallery, quite a successful one too. He bought a coffee, he sat down and read his newspaper.

He looked around and took a liking to one of the pictures. 'I don't recognise the author', he said out loud not really talking to anyone. 'Oh really', I purposely sounded surprised. 'That must be because she's American, very talented too. She doesn't really sell her work around here. I had to travel to USA to get those pictures'.

'I see', he looked at me knowing well I was trying to pull a fast one. 'How much?' he asked. Karina was going to jump in but I squeezed her hand. 'I will give it to you for free', I told him, 'if you put up the rest of them in your gallery'. He laughed and left without a word.

"Oh no." Gabriela was fully engrossed in the story. Adrianna laughed at her reaction.

"I know, that's what Karina said too. She screamed at me for the rest of the day, until the early hours of the morning. 'We could have made some money' she kept repeating but I knew what I was doing the same way she knew when she picked the newspaper few months earlier looking for this place.

"So, he came back the next day. 'You have a deal', he said. '10 pictures for a month'. '20 for three months', I replied. It must have been a lucky day or he liked my persistence but he agreed. He even displayed a couple of them in the window of his gallery. And that's how it all started."

"After a month, he sold the first peace. He brought 50% of the income and put it on the counter. It was more money than we have ever seen."

"What happened then?" Gabriela was hungry for more.

"Then it just started, the coffee, the pictures, the success. Karina bought this place as a thank you few months later. I stayed here doing what I love and she went off to travel the world and do what she loves. But she comes back at least once a year. See," Adrianna picked up her cup. "This stuff is addictive."

"So you helped her?" Gabriela was surprised by the story.

"No, my child," Adrianna touched her face. "We helped each other. Without her there would be no café, no Milan, no man from gallery and without me, well, Karina would make it but it would take her a little longer perhaps. Who knows. If we never met I might have never left my parents' farm."

"That's an amazing story." Gabriela was truly touched Adrianna has shared it with her.

"It is. What are you doing tomorrow?" Adrianna asked.

"Nothing I guess." Gabriela wasn't sure where the question is going.

"OK, you come here tomorrow and you work. You observe, you learn Italian and you learn how to make good coffee."

"I would love that." Gabriela smiled a big, content and hopeful smile.

Noelle

Liam and the boys went away with his parents for the weekend. Noelle was home alone and hungry for some time with Alex. She couldn't stop thinking about her. Not even for a second. She followed her normal routine at home not to make Liam suspicious until she is ready to talk to him.

She kept the same schedule. On Saturdays, they would all get up together, have breakfast and chat about the previous week. She loved hearing the boys talk about school, their friends and first crushes. Liam would take the boys to his parents for the afternoon and that's when she would read a book for a while and go for her walk in a nearby park or the beach.

Alex was always there whenever she texted her. She would drive down to see her. Even if it was just for a few minutes. Once a week they would leave work a little early and go to Alex and spend an evening there. Sometimes they would go out for a few drinks, they would dance, talk for hours without a care in the world.

Their morning coffees before work also became quite a routine. All of it seemed like a stable part of her life now. She found herself with Alex, she found solace in her arms and a burning desire between her legs. She found contentment in her eyes and happiness between their sheets. Sometimes she felt regret that she didn't find her sooner, before Liam, before all this.

At the same time, she couldn't imagine what her world would look without him and she loved her boys. They gave her strength and motivation to keep going when things were hard. When she questioned everything. And she questioned things a lot before she met Alex.

With Alex came peace, answers to questions tormenting her for years and a hope for a simpler future. A future one day she wanted to share with Alex. Even though she didn't know how she is going to get there. She wanted to wake up next to her every day. Start the day looking into those brown eyes.

The trip was planned for a week from today. She would have her big birthday in Poland with Alex which worked out perfect as she didn't want any fuss; no more pretending, no more playing happy family and perfect marriage. She knew this will be a good point to start the conversation with Liam. Once she comes back.

She will have the energy and strength to go ahead with what she planned for the last few months. They will figure out what to tell the boys, she's was going to make sure they are OK. Noelle was going to spend the next afternoon with the boys and Liam before her trip the following Friday but today was free. All for her and Alex.

"Are you free today?" Noelle messaged Alex early that Saturday morning. They already made plans as they had all day and night. She will have to go back early Sunday morning, before they come back, however the next 24 hours where theirs and she wanted to be with Alex as soon as she can. Liam knew she will be working all weekend as usual before any trips, especially when a big new opportunity was just around the corner.

"I'm afraid I'm not," Alex replied. "My boss is making me work all weekend." Another reply and a couple of smiley faces followed.

"What a bitch," Noelle smiled to herself sending this. "We will have to do something about her."

"Well, come over and let me show you what I am going to do."

Noelle felt excited reading this. Her whole body was shook with anticipation, she couldn't wait to see Alex. She couldn't wait to feel her arms around her body and feel her lips on Noelle's lips. She was feeling a warmth between her legs spreading heat all around her body and shivers down her spine.

Noelle jumped in the shower, took a small overnight bag and got into a taxi. She left her car outside the house for the weekend not to cause any suspicion among the neighbours. If anyone asks, she was working all weekend in her office.

Alex and Noelle

Alex set up brunch and waited for Noelle with a big pot of fresh coffee. She had some things planned for them this weekend. She learned, however, to be spontaneous with Noelle. She never knew what Noelle might be in the mood for.

She opened the door wearing a smart casual outfit—jeans, blue shirt and navy jumper. Noelle however seemed to be dressed for a night out already, she came in wearing a black coat and heels.

"It's not that cold is it?" Alex greeted her with a big smile and cheeky comment.

As Noelle made her way to the apartment a tall, good looking brunette walked pass them on the corridor, effortlessly pulling a large suitcase, she lived in an apartment few doors down. She threw them a curious look and got in her apartment leaving them with a seductive smile.

"Who was that?" Noelle asked walking in to Alex's place.

"Would you believe I think it's Gabriela's, well, sort of ex I guess." Noelle looked at her with a confused look.

"The girl from the café. Across from work. She talks to us every morning. Well, she used to she is in Italy now."

"Oh yes I remember." Noelle looked towards the door as if the mysterious woman was still there. "Wow, she has taste."

"She sure does." Alex couldn't wait to unwrap her gift. "So do you." The cheeky smile exposed the dimples and Noelle couldn't resist Alex's charm any longer. She leaned in and put her hands around her.

"What are you in the mood for today?" Alex asked reaching under the coat, she realised Noelle is not wearing anything but a lingerie. Alex could feel her legs getting weaker.

"You," Noelle whispered in to Alex's ear. "I am in the mood for you."

Alex lifted Noelle on the kitchen counter, gently spread her legs and dived in between them. Noelle took off her coat and put her hands on Alex's head, she closed her eyes and gently moved her hips.

Brunch turned into a day in bed. Alex finally got to experience what it would be like to have Noelle as a part of her life. They watched TV and laughed, talked for hours in between sex and just enjoyed each other's company. The evening was approaching and they had a perfect date planned for this perfect weekend.

They got showered and dressed and got into a taxi which brought them to town. Dinner in a cosy Italian restaurant and night club with few drinks before they go back to Alex's place to continue their night. The club was full and different drink promotions were going on, trying them all was something they might later regret.

They enjoyed living in the moment however, as they never knew when the next opportunity for them to be together like this, is going to come around.

"In a week we will be on the plane." Alex was excited and her eyes had that dreamy, hopeful look.

"I know." Noelle gently rubber her cheek. "I will have you all to myself."

"Will we have to go back after that initial week?" Alex never asked Noelle about that, she didn't want to make a big deal of what Katy told her.

"Yes, we will," Noelle smiled. "That was another part of my surprise." She leaned closer and kissed Alex passionately. "We will have to spend around 3 months maybe going back and forth," she continued. "I thought if you want to stay there and I can just fly back and forth and spend as much time with you while I also take care of things here."

"Things?" Alex was hoping she means more than just her business.

"Things. I will have to talk to Liam and well figure out who stays in the house and so on. Let's not talk about that now. There will be time for all of it soon. For you and me." She leaned towards Alex again.

Alex was delighted to hear those words, Noelle was serious and she wanted their life to start. No more hiding, no more sneaking around. Today was a celebration of their relationship and their future together.

"I love you." Noelle looked Alex in the eyes. "This is exciting, I am excited for what the future will bring for the first time in a long time."

"Yea, me too." Alex looked at Noelle. "I love you too. You were worth the risk."

"I guess some risks are worth taking." Noelle laughed and dragged Alex to the dance floor.

They danced for the rest of the night and fell into Alex's apartment drunk on love more than alcohol itself. They woke up the next morning feeling a little worse for wear but extremely happy. Alex was going to make breakfast, she wanted this moment to last as long as possible. Noelle, however, was in a rush to get home. She didn't want to take any chances and get there too late.

She felt guilty for the time she had with Alex and for the love they felt, she felt guilty for lying to Liam. But she knew she can't go back to her life before Alex. She will need to find a way to deal with it for a little longer till she can get the courage to talk to him. To explain.

She looked at Alex making coffee and an overwhelming feeling of love and peace washed over her. She closed her eyes and stayed in the moment. She wanted to hold on to this feeling till Monday morning, until she will see her again. Alex walked her to the door and grabbed her hand.

"I love You Noelle, there is nothing you could do to make me stop loving you." Noelle leaned back and kissed Alex before she went downstairs and got into a taxi. Feeling extremely lucky and even more guilty at the same time.

Noelle

The taxi pulled outside Noelle's house. It was still early, she didn't want to miss Liam's arrival. Noelle got out with a feeling of unease. Liam's car was parked next to hers, the light in the house was on. Her heart started racing and her foggy from last night's prosecco mind was going in circles.

Did they come back early? Did something happen? Surely he would have rang her. Are the boys OK? A spiral of questions hit her head like a speeding train, the only important thought was to check if the twins are ok; she would never forgive herself if something happened and she wasn't there for them. The rest, she can deal with the consequences of her actions as long as the kids are all right.

Noelle approached the door and slowly turned the key; a rush of heat came over her body as she walked into the house, followed by cold sweats. She felt like a teenager breaking a curfew. The house smelled of flowers, lavender candles and roast dinner. A little odd for a Sunday morning she thought.

She put the bag by the door, some part of her hoping no one will notice her, she walked towards the source of smell. Liam was sitting by the kitchen table with a cup of coffee in his hand, roast dinner was laying untouched on the table, the candles still flickering in the back. Balloons with number 40 and congratulations covered the walls.

Noelle felt as if a ton of bricks landed on top of her, she couldn't talk, she couldn't take a step back or forth. Her heart was pounding and so was her head. This isn't how she imagined their talk would start, this was cruel for both of them. Most of all for Liam, he didn't deserve any of this.

"Liam." Noelle finally managed to get some words out of her mouth.

"Don't." Liam didn't even look at her. "Please don't lie to me."

"I won't," she whispered, moving closer to the table. She poured herself a cup of fresh coffee and took a sip in hope this will help her freshen her mind. God I still smell like her she thought. She sat across the table.

"I came back last night, wanted to surprise you," Liam spoke without looking at Noelle. "I was happy you weren't home, you must have went out for a walk I thought. I set up the table and the balloons and started making dinner. Roast lamb, your favourite," he pointed at a joint of meet still sitting untouched on the table. "An hour went by, two, three."

"Why didn't you call me?" She asked as if this was going to make the difference. "Are the boys?"

"The boys are with my parents, they are OK. I thought you have been working so hard and with the trip coming up, I thought we can celebrate your birthday early and well." He looked at Noelle, straight in the eyes, as if he was hoping to find an answer. "Reconnect," he finished. "I thought we can reconnect. But I guess this explains why you were so distant. Why you never wanted," he paused and took a sip of coffee as if to find the courage to finish his sentence.

"Who is he?" He asked.

"It's not like that." Noelle had tears in her eyes. She didn't want him to find out. Not like this. She didn't want to hurt him he didn't deserve it. At this very moment, she felt as if she was losing it all. Could she lose it all?

Was this worth the risk she has been taking for the last few months?

"It's complicated," she finally replied.

"It's not that complicated." His eyes were piercing her soul. "It's simple really. Who is he?" Noelle closed her eyes, she didn't want to lie. Lying was only going to make this worst.

"There is no he," she replied. "I told you it's complicated."

"I know you are hiding something."

"Liam," she took a pause before she continued, slowly. "I am so sorry. I think I'm gay." Liam shook in his chair and a smirk showed on his face.

"Gay?" he asked in disbelief. "How can you be gay? You are married to me and we have two kids. You are not gay."

"Please don't dismiss what I'm feeling."

"I'm not," Liam got serious again, he looked relieved somehow. "OK, is this why, you know. We weren't physical of late?" His eyes teared up. "Did you force yourself to? You know be with me? Did I ever hurt you?" Thoughts were now rushing through his head. "I would never if I had known."

"No, Liam no." Noelle moved closer and touched his hand. "You didn't. I love you." He looked at her with hope in his eyes.

"It's ok," Liam whispered putting his head on her arm. "We can work through this. I mean whatever you need." Noelle closed her eyes. She felt relieved as if a weight has been lifted off her shoulders. What did she want? What did she want to do next was a mystery to both of them.

"I don't know what I need, Liam." He looked up.

"Do you want to, I don't know, experiment? See if this is really what you want? You know society," he continued, "you have a life, a status, people might not accept you. I don't want anyone to," he took a pause to collect his thoughts. "You know it's not easy coming out. Especially late in life and what about the boys? And school? Parents and teachers, we will do whatever you want. Just tell me what you need? Can we not tell people? Maybe stay here and we will just live as normal."

"You want me to have a double life?" Noelle wasn't sure what he meant. They didn't make any decisions yet he was jumping to conclusions.

"I want you to be happy. I will fight for us with everything I have. But if," he looked at Noelle. "If that's what it is than there is nothing I can do is there? The only thing I can do is to protect you from people, from judgement."

Even in this moment he didn't think about himself. He thought about her, about the shame, the society's judgement, the impact on their kids and her status, their families, friends. The life they build together was possibly falling apart and all he could think about was her. She understood why she fell in love with him years ago and even now she still loved him with all her heart. She also loved Alex. Could you love two people at the same time, she asked herself.

It must have been an hour later by the time they stood up from the table. They both knew nothing will change straight away. Noelle knew she needs to figure out what to do next. What does she want in her life and is she brave and ready to make the changes she will need to make, was she courageous enough to show the world who she really is, risk everything?

Her family, friends, her company. There was so much on the line. On one hand what she felt for Alex was something she never felt before, who she was around her, no pretending, no lying to herself. On the other however, her whole life was going to fall apart.

Everything she build, everything they build together was hanging on a promise from a stranger. A promise of love she didn't even know she will ever be fully ready for.

Karina

Karina arrived home early in the afternoon. She didn't want to be away any longer, she missed her Dublin apartment. Between the contract work in Greece and her stay in Italy, her new exhibition was ready. She had enough going on in Dublin and the most important and anticipated, opening of the new gallery she wanted to stay here for a bit and make sure everything is going according to plan.

She was a perfectionist on all fronts, her work, her appearance her apartment. Everything around her and about her was perfect. And she liked it that way. She poured herself a glass of red wine and opened all of the windows in the apartment.

She loved the breeze of fresh, sea air and sound of sea gulls. She started unpacking only to get interrupted by a sound of incoming call.

"Miss me already?" she answered playfully.

"Your friend is doing well." Adriana got straight to the point. "She is a sweet and innocent girl. I'm glad you didn't completely corrupt her." She laughed.

"I am glad to hear that." Karina smiled to herself. "Thank you."

"Oh no, thank you, she is a good kid. I'm happy to help." Adriana continued. "And she is quite entertaining."

"She is, isn't she." Karina was glad she was able to help Gabriela; she felt bad for hurting her.

"You doing OK?"

"Yes," Karina answered. "I am great actually."

"Good, have to run now. Call you tomorrow." Adriana hung up before Karina was able to say anything. She put down her phone and carried on with the chore of unpacking.

The fresh bags of coffee brough a smile to her face, a couple of bottles of good Italian wine. She stocked up on all of her favourites, with all the grandeur and sophistication in her life she really cherished the small things the most. She put on a slow jazz record and dimmed the lights. She closed her eyes, took a deep breath and enjoyed the moment.

She enjoyed some peace and quiet after all the excitement of the last few weeks. She knew this won't last too long as she had a lot to do over the next few months in order to get to where she wants to be. Even at a peak of her success she never stopped for a moment, never took time to just appreciate what she has achieved, acknowledge how far she has come.

Her drive is what got her here and her drive is what kept her going forward. She took out her journal however, and with a smile on her face she ticked little perfectly shaped boxes next to a couple of goals she wrote out before. Everything in her life was going according to her plan, no disruptions, no surprises. Her determination and discipline have never failed her but most of all her faith that all of this was possible.

She looked at the end of the page, she smiled before she closed the page. One little tiny box not filled yet. She must have wrote it years ago when she was still naïve, young and silly. The last box, somehow forgotten. She completely lost hope for it but made peace with. The last box said.

Fall in Love!

In some way, she fell in love each and every day. She fell in love with her life, her art, her friends and the perfect glass of red wine she was holding in her hand. Maybe falling in love is not what the society tells little girls it must be. Like happiness itself, she knew happiness is what she wants to feel each and every day, it's not a destination. Maybe it's the same with love.

Alex

Alex rushed into the office that Monday morning. She didn't hear from Noelle since she left her apartment on Sunday morning. It was not like Noelle to not make any contact. No text, no pin, no Instagram post, nothing.

So many scenarios played in her head. Did something happened on Sunday, did she tell Liam, did he do something. Alex knew Noelle is going to tell him at some point. Not hearing from her, not seeing her in the office, it made her feel uneasy.

Alex was getting worried she knew however, she can't reach out. She was going to give it another while before she texts her. At the end of the day, the trip was coming up in a few days and they were going to finally be by themselves.

Finally, be free to express their love and start planning for their future and life together. Alex tried to focus on the positive, she did her best to chase the dark thoughts away and focus on the plans they put in place.

"Noelle won't be in today. I think one of the boys caught a bug." Katy stuck her head into the door and broke Alex's train of thought. Thankfully.

"Hi, Katy, nice to see you too." Alex laughed

"Oh." Katy blushed as she walked into Alex's new office. "Hi, Alex." She started over. "Noelle just rang she won't be in today. She said to go ahead with the meetings and plans for the trip and she will call you when she can."

"Great," Alex felt relieved. "Thank you, we can talk later about the details if that's OK."

"Of course," Katy seemed eager to be of service. "Should we organise a little celebratory party before you guys go?"

"No, I don't think that will be necessary." Alex didn't want to take any chances, all she wanted is to get on that plane and make sure all goes to plan. She noticed Katy's disappointment. "Maybe in a week when we are back." She smiled. "Once we actually have something to celebrate!"

"Right," Katy smiled back. "That's a much better idea." She left the office with excitement in her eyes.

Alex didn't hear from Noelle till later in the week. She knew something was going on, however there was nothing she could have done without causing a scene or drama so she decided to keep it cool and wait for Noelle to reach out. She knew she will as soon as she can.

Her phone rang.

"Hi, I'm downstairs." Noelle seemed rushed.

"Coming." Alex was so excited to finally see her. It seemed to take forever but Noelle finally appeared out of the elevator.

She jumped into Alex's arms and stayed there for a couple of long minutes.

"Is everything OK?" Alex asked.

"He knows," Noelle whispered as if she didn't want anyone to hear.

"Are you OK? Did he?" Alex felt helpless.

"No, he would never. He is so loving and caring. He worries about me, about what our family will say, the kids."

"Noelle," Alex stopped her. "It doesn't really matter what he thinks, does it? You know what you want and what you feel. It's about what you want. Everything else will fall into place. I promise." Alex smiled that soft, loving, endearing smile Noelle fell for.

"I want you." Noelle kissed Alex.

"Good, I want us too." Alex tried to lighten the mood. She knew, however, there is nothing she can do other than support Noelle. She has to go through this herself.

"I don't want to hurt him, or the kids." Noelle looked Alex in the eyes.

"I know, everything and everyone will be OK. Just don't hurt yourself either."

"I won't."

"The trip is in three days." Alex didn't want to push Noelle, however she wanted this so much. It's what they were waiting for the last couple of weeks. The idea of being away from everything and everyone. Just the two of them.

"I know," Noelle looked down.

"It's going to be OK." Alex took Noelle in her arms again and gave her a warm embrace. "I know it seems crazy right now but maybe the timing is just perfect; you know things often happen the way they are supposed to. Everything is out in the open, you don't have to hide or worry.

"We can go away, it will give you some time to think and it will give you strength to deal with things when you come back." Noelle looked at Alex. She gave her strength, her warmth and understanding was soothing and encouraging.

"You are right." She felt more confident. "Maybe it's just what we both need. I will have to talk to Liam, one of us will have to move out. We will need to talk to the kids. I will do that when we come back."

"Do whatever feels right." Alex was gentle and not demanding however, firm. Noelle knew this is where she needs to make decisions. Things happened, maybe for a reason and she needs to just take of the band-aid. "I will talk to Liam when we get back." She looked at her phone. "I have to go now."

"OK." Alex gave Noelle a kiss and a big hug. "You will be OK, everything will work out I promise."

"I know," Noelle moved towards the door. "I will call you before the flight and will probably meet you at the airport. Just give me a day or two to sort this out."

"No problem."

The door closed and Noelle disappeared back into the elevator. Alex was relieved but also unsettled. She didn't know why but she felt sad. Things were coming to an end and things were starting.

She has changed her own life so much over the last few months and even weeks really. She didn't have a chance to sit back and reflect. She was glad it will soon start to slow down. She took off her clothes and took a long, hot shower. She hoped it will stop her mind from the overdrive she felt over the last few days.

Gabriela

It was another sunny day in Milan, everything here seemed better. The sun shined brighter, the birds chirped more cheerfully, the clouds had that perfectly white, fluffy look. Like candy floss high up in the sky held by some magical powers.

The only word that over and over came to Gabriela's mind as she tried to understand the beauty and power of this place was—it was pure magic. She looked at *The Secret* lying next to her bed at the bedside table. She finished it last night and started thinking about the last few months. Since she started reading it back in her bedroom which she shared with two friends.

She wanted more from life, she wanted to experience love, adventures, she wasn't looking for a fairy tale but it found her, instead of giving her a happy ending it broke her heart but that heart break brought her here. There was a small apartment on top of the café, it was empty, so Adrianna told Gabriela she can move in. It wasn't much but she loved it. The constant smell of fresh coffee coming from downstairs was only one of the perks.

She loved sitting in the window, she could see the street below and just spend hours watching life go by. She fell in love with the streets of Milan, with this little café below her and the people that came in and out. She fell in love with Italy and now working for Adrianna she was able to stay here. Not to mention her own place in the world, her own little piece of heaven she always dreamed of.

It's funny how life works, she often thought to herself not really knowing if the book had anything to do with everything that happened in her life. Was this her happy ending? Was this her dream come true? Was this life what she always wanted? A lot of questions came to her mind, however she found peace and didn't want to give in to her constantly overactive mind.

She worked in the café, she read books in her spare time, she walked around Milan and for the first time in a long time she felt she belonged. She didn't miss Dublin as much as she thought she would. This was her new home. Possibly her forever home. Her Italian was coming along nicely, she learned every day and Adrianna forbid her from speaking English to customers.

She didn't take her seriously but knew she means well, so Gabriela listened and it helped improve her language. Another thing she was grateful for. Gabriela looked at the time, it was close to her shift and she didn't want to be late. She opened her laptop however, and quickly wrote in her blog:

'I came here to find answers from someone who once broke my heart, what I found instead is home, peace and hope for the future. If you close yourself to forgiveness you might close yourself to an amazing opportunity. If your life is driven by hate and resentment your heart will close to love and kindness.

'Always find something to be grateful for in any situation, always find something to appreciate and the world, life might surprise you with a gift beyond your wildest dreams. Stay grateful my friends.'

Yours Truly
G.

Noelle

Noelle sat down on the bench in her back garden with a glass of red wine. It was chilly but she didn't seem to be bothered. She put on a fire in a little outdoor metal fire pit. The flight was tomorrow. She told Katy to make the arrangements for the change of plans, she didn't talk to Alex yet.

She knew she has to call her and she knew Alex will understand. She wanted to do it in person but she didn't get a chance to leave the house for long enough. Not with everything going on. Liam took the boys to their swimming class, it gave Noelle some time to be on her own, collect her thoughts and make the call.

Her and Liam spend the last week talking, possibly more than over the last few years. They went for walks, talked about the changes they need to make. They both cried and they laughed remembering things from the past. Noelle was glad she can lean on him even under these circumstances, it made her sad also that she needs to give it all up.

She missed Alex with every fibre of her body, however now was not the time to start their future together. Noelle wanted a clean break before she jumps into creating a new life with the woman she loves so much. She picked up the phone and with a heavy heart made the call.

"Hello," Alex's warm voice made it even harder.

"Hi, honey," Noelle tried to keep it light even though she knew she will disappoint Alex. "I am so sorry I can't go with you tomorrow."

"I had a feeling." Just as Noelle thought Alex was nothing but understanding. "Are you OK?" Alex asked concerned.

"I'm fine," Noelle paused. "I am so sorry. I can't see you before the flight. I promise I will make it up to you. I will take this week and figure things out. I have a viewing tomorrow, I think I will get an apartment close to yours.

"I would like a clean break. Something new. Liam has been great, very supportive."

"That's good." Alex wasn't sure how to react to this information. All she wanted is to get on the plane tomorrow, with Noelle by her side. She was willing to wait, she was patient and understanding and knew the changes Noelle was going to make will not happen overnight.

"I miss you," Alex tried her best to keep the call somewhat positive. "I am really glad that you're OK and well that things are moving forward. Do what you have to do and we can chat properly next week."

"I would love that." Noelle heard the key in the door. "Alex, I'm so sorry. I have to go. I love you." She hung up before Alex was able to say the same.

Alex

The silence on the other side of the call summed up what Alex felt in this very moment. Somehow she knew things are not going to happen like planned. The overwhelming feeling of sadness took over, a feeling she fought so hard to keep out since the start of the week. What was supposed to be a start of their life together ended up crashing before it had a chance to flourish.

Alex tried not to let her mind go to the worst case scenario. Everything is OK, Noelle is getting some things sorted, she told herself. She was patient for the last few months, she can be patient for a little while longer. They both need to. Having a distraction with work and seeing her friends and family will be good for her, she knew that.

Being around people who love her unconditionally after all the changes she made in her life. Only now she realised how much her life has changed. She was happy, however she never really processed her split from Niamh. 7 years of a relationship gone in a couple of days.

She didn't see Niamh since she moved out and collected all her stuff. She also never saw any of their mutual friends. She was OK with it; she made her choices, faced the consequences and was happy with her life. She never really processed the loss and all of the adjustments in her life. It all seemed to be pouring into her head now.

She started crying, uncontrollably. She was glad no one was in the office at this hour. She looked for tissues but couldn't find any. She walked out of the office and headed towards the bathroom when she heard a voice behind her.

"Are you OK?" Katy sounded concerned.

"Oh I'm sorry. I didn't know you were here." Alex felt embarrassed.

"It's OK. Are you OK?" Katy looked at Alex and put her arms around her. "Whatever is happening you can talk to me," she added.

"I'm OK." Alex wasn't able to talk, she gave into Katy's warm embrace. It gave her comfort. "What are you doing here anyway," she finally managed to swallow back the tears.

"Oh, I was changing the bookings for the trip tomorrow. Noelle can't make it due to her kid being sick, so she asked me to step in. I think they made a mistake in the hotel reservation as you only had one room so I made changes."

"Ah great, thanks." Alex felt too close for comfort, she didn't want them to get caught, not now as it will only complicate an already messy situation. She didn't know Katy was coming instead and the whole hotel mix up was leaving them exposed. "I was going to stay with my family." Alex thought of a quick excuse. "That's why the one room," she smiled.

"Oh, I'm so sorry," Katy blushed. "Should I change the…"

"No, no," Alex said before she was able to finish the sentence. "Having my own space might be nice actually. I haven't been home in a long time."

"It might get overwhelming." Katy smiled. "Is that why you got upset?"

"Something like that." Alex felt a little better. She smiled back at Katy. "Thank you. I'm OK now."

"OK, I will go and pack. You should probably get home and do the same. I will see you tomorrow?"

"Yes, see you at the airport."

Alex went back to the office to collect her laptop. She felt embarrassed, she didn't think anyone will see her. She also felt a little relieved Katy will be there. From all the people in the office, she was the easiest to talk to and a little fun. Alex started feeling slightly better knowing she will not have to look at an empty seat tomorrow morning.

*****

Poland was unusually sunny this time of the year, cold but sunny. Some promise of snow excited Katy. Alex was a good sport she tried to keep up with the conversations, answer many questions and keep the positive spirit of the journey even though the only thing she wanted was to be on her own. She looked at her phone over and over.

Noelle came down this morning and dropped her to the airport, risky but extremely positive surprise. Alex was holding back the tears during their morning conversation and gave Noelle a long, soft kiss. In some way, it felt as if it was the last. The last under those circumstances.

By the time she comes back to Dublin, Noelle will have a lease on her apartment and they will be able to make plans for the start of their relationship. A bitter sweet feeling was a theme of the week for Alex. The flight landed on time and a taxi dropped them to a hotel, two rooms. Thank god Katy checked and changed the reservation as this could have been really awkward, Alex thought.

"Do you want to grab lunch or show me around town?" Katy asked still super excited.

"I was thinking about going to my family." Alex wanted to be alone. "You know what I can go there tomorrow," seeing disappointment on Katy's face softened Alex.

"Are you sure? I don't want you to change your plans."

"No, it's ok," Alex smiled. "I can hang out with you today. Show you around. I will spend the weekend with my family, so book some spa treatments and treat yourself and we can start first thing Monday morning?" Alex was hoping this will be OK for Katy.

"Absolutely." Katy was happy and excited at the idea of the weekend full of treats for herself. "See you in a while," she said before she disappeared in her room.

Alex walked into the room just when the phone rang. It was Noelle, she smiled as she answered the phone.

"I miss you."

"I miss you too," Noelle answered. "Again, I'm really sorry it had to be this way. I have a viewing later on today and will talk to Liam after. I will do my best to collect you next week and maybe bring you well to our new place."

"Our ha?" Alex was a little surprised.

"Well," Noelle chuckled. "It will be one day. Right?" She asked.

"I would love nothing more." Alex was so happy in this moment.

Even if the trip didn't work out things were moving forward and Noelle did what she promised. She just needs to hold on for one week and they will be together again. Noelle will be in her arms, where she belongs. "How are you feeling?"

"I'm OK, things are well," Noelle took a moment. "A little bitter sweet to be honest but I'm OK, and I love you."

"I love you too. Katy is waiting for me downstairs. I promised to take her out and show her around town." Alex was sad she had to go she knew however, Noelle only has few minutes anyway.

"That's OK, have fun and I will call you tomorrow evening."

"I'm looking forward to it."

The very quick conversation gave Alex all the reassurance she needed. She knew Noelle will move forward however, she didn't know if it will all happen so soon. She never pushed her to do anything and her patience was finally paying off.

With a big smile on her face Alex walked into the lobby, for the first time she was able to match Katy's excitement.

"Ready?" She asked as they moved towards the entrance.

Noelle

Noelle came downstairs and looked at the boys. So happy, so innocent, so unaware of what was going on around them. She didn't want to break their little hearts; she couldn't however go on the way things were. Not anymore, she knew who she is and she knew what she wants for the first time in her life.

She needed to talk to Liam and figure this out together. Her appointment was in two hours. She felt a pain in her heart thinking about moving the boys to a new place. They loved the house, they had so many friends here and a school nearby.

All of a sudden she started questioning her decisions. Liam came down the stairs. He has lost so much weight in a space of a week. She didn't think he neither slept or ate. She felt so bad looking at his sad, hurt face.

"Are you OK?" she asked and instantly regretted it.

"Are you serious?" he replied. "My marriages is," he took a pause. "Well, I don't actually know what's happening. I just feel I'm losing you. I can't lose you, or the boys."

"You won't lose the boys." She assured him with a warm smile. Noelle walked over and gave him a hug. "They adore you, I would never do anything to hurt your relationship with them, you know that."

"I know you wouldn't." Liam held on to the hug. "I'm sorry."

"No, don't." Noelle rubbed the tears from his cheeks. "I am sorry. I never wanted any of this. I never wanted it to go this way. I just…"

"You just?"

"I don't know. I just need change."

"Change?" Liam was getting impatient. "You can change shoes, or a car or a house not a family not a marriage after 20 years. What change do you want?"

Noelle knew he was entitled to ask that questions. She found it hard to explain what she feels without telling him about Alex, she couldn't do that to him. She didn't want him to know.

"I asked you to go and explore; go out there and try whatever you need to try. Get it out of your system, see if it's worth changing your life for," he continued.

"I can't do that," Noelle replied. "Please stop. We need to talk about the boys. I am going to look at an apartment today."

"What do you mean?" He seemed surprised.

"I need to move out Liam, give you space and time to heal."

"You can't take the boys from here, it's their home."

"Well, I didn't figure that one out yet."

"Look," Liam was once again the focused and calm man she married. "Doesn't matter what is going on between us, the boys need to stay here. I understand you need space that's OK. We do a rota and figure this out.

"Whoever is with the boys stays here and we can both rent something in the meantime. I can stay with my parents."

"Is that what you want?" Noelle asked surprised.

"It's not what I want. I want my family to stay together. Always." He smiled. "It's what's right. I will start working in my brother's company also. I need to get back out there."

"That's not necessary, we have more than enough I don't want you do have to do anything drastic."

"You have more than enough." The look on his face changed from kind to serious. "I need to start looking after myself."

"Liam," Noelle touched his hands. "We build this together. You supported me since I was 19, you stayed home with the kids so I can run my business. Whatever it makes its as much yours as it is mine. You know that right?"

"Thank you," Liam smiled. "I have to do this for me."

"Whatever you want." Noelle hated herself for doing this to him, to the boys, to their family. She never really thought of the consequences of her decisions. She couldn't however live a lie. Her feelings for Alex were too strong.

"I have to…"

"I know, go and we can continue when you get back."

She got into the car and drove off. She felt relieved after Liam's solution to keep the boys in the house. She was glad she doesn't have to rip them from their routine, their life. She never thought of this herself but that's why she knew she can always rely on Liam, he always made the most calculated and smart choices.

In a way, he was her rock, she forgot about it over the years. She arrived at the apartment. She realised she won't need a 3 bed anymore. Actually, she didn't need anything. She can just move in with Alex, and go back to the house when she's with the boys.

That should work better than having two separate places anyway. That way they can just be together, all the time. She never thought about the pain she was causing and the pain she was still going to cause. For the last few months, she only focused on the pleasure she was feeling, on the new experiences she was exploring, the love, the feeling of being understood and the peace it brought to her life.

All of a sudden she started thinking about the last few months. How good it felt to be herself for the first time in her life, she felt gratitude towards what she had with Alex. Was it enough however for her to change her whole life? Throw away everything she ever worked for? She felt confused. The agent knocked on the window.

"Hi, are you ready?"

The apartment was beautiful. She never told the estate agent she won't actually need it. She thought a little distraction might do her good. Also being there, imagining her and Alex together, sitting on the sofa and watching TV, playing in the bedroom, taking a shower or a bath together. She could see Alex pouring them a glass of wine by the kitchen island.

She could see them trying out new recipes, laughing, kissing. She could imagine quite clearly what it would be like to be there with Alex. To start the new chapter of her life. The extra bedrooms were also beautiful, nearly as big as the master.

All of the sudden, it started to feel empty. She could now see Liam sitting in the arm chair reading a book, boys watching cartoons, playing, arguing and spilling paint all over the floor. It put a smile on her face, she closed her eyes. The silence hit her like a speeding train. She opened her eyes, all the images were gone.

It was just her. Standing in an empty space, cold and cruel. Just like she has been towards her family over the last while. Overindulging in her own pleasure, not being able to fight the desire that burned under her skin. She walked out of the apartment and got back in the car.

She barely made it before a sea of tears poured down her cheeks. She didn't cry in years, not like this. She couldn't stop it. She sat in the car with one thought racing through her mind. What have I done?

Alex

Alex came back into her luxurious and spacious hotel room after breakfast. She promised Katy she will join her before they both go their own ways for the rest of the weekend. She sat on the bed and looked around the room. She liked the feature of glass wall around the bathroom.

She thought how she would enjoy being here with Noelle, the plan they had previously made together. She could just lie here and look at her take a shower. She looked at the large window overlooking the city and the soft, wide seats spread across its length.

Another idea popped into her head. Every time she closed her eyes she saw Noelle, she felt her presence. Even thought they were never here together they talked about it so often, they imagined how it would feel, what they would do, those conversations played in Alex's mind leaving her feeling disappointed. She didn't however have time to feel sorry for herself.

Her family and friends were coming over tonight and she was looking forward to catching up with everyone. She jumped in the shower, put on nice, fresh clothes and a big smile on her face and was soon ready to conquer the world. She hoped her eyes won't betray her tonight and she can stay in good spirit and enjoy a company of some good old friends.

She arrived at her mom's apartment and was glad to get a long, loving hug. A hug she didn't know she missed until this moment. Her eyes filled up with tears and no matter how much she tried to hold back she couldn't. She cried, and then cried some more. Just like back when she was a 5 year old girl and scraped her knee, back then however, all she needed was her mom's hug this time as comforting as it was it did not bring the solutions to any of her hearts desires.

Alex calmed down after a while, she couldn't explain the outburst; her mom didn't need any explanation. She knew all that was going on and wanted her daughter to relax and forget about her problems. "Things always find a way to work themselves out," was the only thing she said.

Alex fixed her red face and didn't try to figure out what happened. Her friends arrived, more hugs followed and they all sat down to a feast, she could always count on her mom for that. The table covered in various dishes and wines. It was heart-warming looking at the faces of her friends, most with husbands and kids.

She knew them since they were 15, and nearly 20 years later, they shared a special bond. Sometimes years would pass in which they wouldn't see each other but as soon as they did it felt as if the time stopped. For a couple of hours, every few years they would all feel 18 again.

The giggles around the table reminded Alex of a simpler time. The time their only problem was to figure out what to wear to a party. It all seemed so trivial, however those memories were precious. Alex thought about all the decisions and choices she has made that brought her to where she is now.

She was happy and proud. She loved who she became and really enjoyed her last few months. Her freedom, the ability to be herself. The only thing on her mind was Noelle and the questions as to what is going to happen next. She wanted them to start their life together more than anything in the world.

The evening was slowly coming to an end and even thought her friends could see Alex was distracted and often looking at her phone they didn't say anything. They knew each other well and knew when to ask questions and when to wait till she is read to talk. Her phone rang and she apologised and sneaked out to another room.

She knew this probably won't take long, she was yearning to hear Noelle's voice all day and didn't want to miss what might have been her only opportunity to talk to her.

"Hi," Alex answered cheerfully. All of her worries and doubts dispersed.

"Hi, did you get to your mom's OK?" Noelle asked.

"Yes, I have."

"That's good." Noelle sounded relieved. "You need that, you know to be around your family and friends."

"I guess I did." Alex couldn't wait to hear about how the viewing went, she didn't want to rush Noelle. "How are you?"

"I'm good, I did some thinking and you know."

"Oh yea, what did you think about?"

"I had a think about what I am doing, to my life and my family."

"What do you mean?" Alex was confused.

"Alex, I love you so much. I want to be with you and nothing will change between us. I can't move out from my home. I can't leave the kids."

"You don't have to leave your kids. That was never an issue."

"No, I know." Noelle seemed all over the place. "It's too much for me. Too many changes. I can't do it that way, not right now. For my own mental health, I need to stay home. Everything is changing so fast. We have made so many decisions so fast."

"Noelle, you made those decisions, I have never pushed you to do anything."

"I know," Noelle caught her breath. "I know you are the sweetest and I am sorry I just can't do this right now."

"And you waited to tell me this when I am on a different continent?" Alex didn't know what to say, what to think, what to feel.

"I am sorry, I really am. You know I love you. It just all feels so quick, so sudden I feel like too many things are changing."

"I understand." Alex took a step back. "Look just take it easy and mind yourself. We can talk when I get back."

"I would like that. I'm sorry I have to go now."

"Of course you do." Alex wasn't surprised Noelle dropped such news on her and had to go straight after.

"I love you," Noelle whispered.

"I love you too." Alex listened to the silence on the other side of the phone for a few min. She knew she has to gather her thoughts and join her guests waiting in the other room, she needed to pretend everything is OK. More for herself than anyone else.

A couple of hours later everyone was gone. Alex helped her mom clean up, a while later they went for a walk with the dogs. Alex knew some fresh air will do her good, it should clear her mind. She had such a busy week and schedule ahead of her the last thing she needed was to be preoccupied with Noelle's news.

She knew she can confine in her Mom and always count on a good advice so that's what she did. She told her about all the promises, all the plans and then the call that came tonight. After she finished she felt like the space around her is getting smaller, her chest got tighter, she couldn't walk or breath. She stood underneath a tree and supported herself with one hand, her dinner, drinks all came rushing out of her underneath the tree.

Her mind was spinning, her stomach was sick and her heart was in so much pain, she never thought she can physically feel so much pain from a broken heart.

She was embarrassed her mom had to witness this, however from all the people in the world, she was glad it was her mom.

"Oh, darling," her mom finally spoke once Alex's breath came back to normal. "No one, and I mean no one is worth this amount of pain. Give yourself 24 hours and get over whatever you are feeling right now. As long as both of you are alive, you can change things.

"You can talk, you can figure things out, and if you think this will cause you nothing but pain, you need to move on as painful as it will be at that moment keeping it going like this is not worth it."

"I need to let her go," Alex whispered painfully as they walked back towards the house. The pain she felt was not because of what Noelle said, the pain she felt was from a realisation that she might never be ready or brave enough to change her life. Alex understood how hard it must have been for her discovering the truth about herself at this stage of her life.

At the stage where you think you know everything about yourself. She was not willing however, to waste any of her own life waiting for someone who might never be ready. And that's why her whole body was shaking with pain.

*****

The pain didn't leave that week, it was going to stay there for a while. Maybe a month, maybe more; however Alex was nothing but professional and pragmatic. She had the ability to always put her emotions aside and practically calculate her best and worst case scenario.

She took the Sunday to think and weigh her options with Noelle; what her heart wanted was one thing however she trusted her head and her gut. She wanted nothing more in the world to just believe that Noelle will one day be ready, she wasn't however, willing to take that gamble with her own time and life. All week Alex showed up to work on time.

She delivered her tasks to the highest standards and as nervous as she was doing some of it for the first time, she was happy she could rely on Katy's experience and positive attitude. She put her emotions and pain aside and did what she was there to do. Set up a new branch, first HQ in eastern Europe. The business was expanding and she was happy she was the one who made it happen.

Friday came rather quickly and the flight back seemed like a good idea to celebrate. Alex and Katy had a couple of drinks and talked about the success this trip surely was.

"Are you going back next week?" Katy asked.

"Going back?" Alex was a little confused, she completely forgot about that.

"Oh, to Poland. Normally when we open a new branch it takes a couple of months to get things going. Noelle likes one of the Senior Managers to oversee it themselves."

"How long does that normally take?"

"Normally, 3 to 6 months. I am sorry," Katy felt like she was overstepping. "I didn't mean to."

"It's OK." Alex smiled to give her some comfort. "I just might."

The plane was landing shortly. Alex closed her eyes and smiled. 3 months away from all this might just be what she needed. She will be able to clear her head, focus on work, see her family. It will also give Noelle the time she needs to figure out what she wants. Just like her mom said, everything always works itself out.

Noelle

Noelle knew the plane has landed. She was checking the air scanner for the last hour. She was supposed to collect Alex and bring her home, then stay the night. All those plans have changed now. Even if she wanted to just drop her home and see her she couldn't find a good enough excuse to leave home late on a Friday night.

She missed Alex, but the guilt she felt was stronger. The shame she felt was not easy to shake off. For the first time in months, she felt all the questions from the past flooding back into her mind. Those voices disappeared when she met Alex, when their affair started, when she felt her lovers grip around her waist for the first time.

As if Alex's touch was magic, it made all the doubts disappear. It made her feel home. There was more at stake than her selfish needs however, and Noelle felt angry at herself for reminiscing about Alex's touch. She wanted to be normal.

She wanted to feel the desire for her husband and contentment with what they build over the years, however all she could think of were Alex's lips and her beautiful brown eyes. She took out her phone and texted while she was in the bathroom.

"I'm so sorry I can't collect you. I will met you tomorrow for a coffee."

She couldn't wait for the next day. She needed to see Alex, to explain. Even though she went to bed early, she tossed and turned most of the night; the morning couldn't come fast enough. Fed up with the clock watching, Noelle got up earlier than normal, made breakfast for everyone and spend some time with the boys.

She enjoyed their company and felt she wasn't there for them lately. She wanted to overcompensate and make her guilt this tiny bit smaller before she goes off to meet her lover. Juggling running a successful business, being a mother, wife and realising what is beneath it all, for once in her life feeding her own deepest desires, all of it took a toll on her.

Liam looked happy for the first time in a long time. In his world, the turbulence of the past few weeks were now gone. He was able to move on knowing Noelle changed her mind. He knew her so well. He knew every now and then she obsesses about something, finds a new trend in cooking or exercise, intermitting fasting.

Things always come and go and in his mind this was just one of those things. He kissed her on a cheek and told the boys to get ready. Just as every weekend, he was taking them for brunch to his parents. In his world, everything was the same, everything was back to normal.

In hers, however, it couldn't be further from the truth. Noelle waited for Liam and the boys to leave before she took a shower, she put on jeans and a Levi's T-shirt. She wanted to look casual but nice. She told Liam she has to pop into the office which bought her some extra time she could spend with Alex.

She got into the car and drove to the office where she left the car in the parking lot. Everything was perfectly planned and coordinated. She knew what she was doing and became a master of alibi over the last while, something she wasn't too proud of, however it came in handy and kept her out of trouble and suspicion.

Alex's apartment was nearby she didn't want to go there. She knew she won't be able to resist her if they are in the same space with no one around. Coffee shop was a safer option. Noelle walked in; she was happy to see Alex after a week. She was a little afraid of Alex's reaction to the news she gave her over the phone, at the same time she was glad she has delivered them already.

Alex was there ordering their coffee. It brought a smile to Noelle's face. Her fear that things will change between them was put to ease. Alex wore black Chelsea boots and black jeans with ripped knees, black tight jumper and a black coat.

She looked so good with her hair freshly styled, flawlessly falling down pass her shoulders. Noelle felt lucky to have her in her life.

"Hi." Noelle walked towards Alex with a big smile on her face.

"Hi." Alex was a little withdrawn, surely all will be OK once they talk.

They took the coffee and walked towards the door leading upstairs to their favourite couch. It was Saturday and with the surrounding offices being empty it shouldn't be busy, Noelle wanted to have Alex all to herself after the absence last week.

She couldn't help herself once they reached the camera free spot on the stairs. "Hey," she whispered. Alex stopped and looked back. Noelle pushed Alex's body against the wall and kissed her passionately. Oh how she missed those sweet, plump lips. Alex didn't resist. She wanted to but couldn't.

She didn't know if she will ever feel Noelle's lips on hers again, and right now she enjoyed the dopamine kick hitting every cell in her body. Noelle was like a drug, she knew she shouldn't indulge but the craving was too hard to resist. They kissed for longer than usual, both hungry for more than each other's company.

The pain Alex felt lifted with that one kiss. Is it possible to maintain this relationship? Keep what they have? They heard the door open downstairs and rushed upstairs. Just like Noelle thought, there was no one there. They sat comfortably on their favourite brown leather sofa in the middle of the room.

"I'm so happy to see you," Noelle smiled.

"What happened?" Alex was confused. She felt bad she has already made a decision as to how this relationship should go, how it should end. Noelle behave as if nothing ever happened. Maybe Alex misunderstood her, maybe things are as they were before she left.

"What happened with?"

"The apartment."

"Oh," Noelle seemed surprised by the question. She was hoping they won't talk about her sudden change of plans. "I'm really sorry, Alex, I am. I just can't do this right now. I can't just pack and leave and pretend the last 20 years of my life doesn't mean anything."

"I never asked you to do that." Alex moved closer and put her hand on Noelle's leg. "The last 20 years helped you to realise who you are, they helped you create what you have. It is not a wasted time quite the opposite." She smiled that sweet, beautiful smile which always put Noelle at ease.

"You didn't know who you were, what you wanted and desired. Now you know and based on that some things have changed. What you are doing is creating your future not erasing your past."

"You are right." Noelle put her hand on Alex's hand. "I just can't quite move on, not like this. I want to keep seeing you, I just can't move out from my home or…" she paused.

"Or?" Alex wasn't sure where this was going.

"Or leave Liam," she whispered.

"You don't want to leave your husband?" Alex felt a sharp pain as if a dagger pierced her right in the middle of her chest. "Would you like to come to my place so we can talk properly."

"You know I can't," Noelle replied.

"I don't know, Noelle. I don't really know what you want me to do with all this information. With all those decisions you have made in a space of a week."

"Alex, you don't understand." Noelle seemed upset, she shifted in her seat nervously. This was the first time Alex questioned her.

"I understand." Alex's eyes were still full of love for her but she seemed a little distant. "I understand perfectly. You build a life with someone, you lived that life because you didn't know anything else. But there was a little spark burning inside you. At first just barely visible, you couldn't really feel it and it would remind you of its existence every so often. Over the years, however, that spark became larger, it started burning stronger. It would call out more often, from once in a few months to nearly every day. That spark of desire became so intense and extreme you could no longer ignore it.

You could no longer hide it, it took over your whole existence. You didn't quite understand what it wants, what it feeds of. Until one day, it all became clear. One day you realised what it was and you finally allowed yourself to give in. You have indulged, you felt something has changed.

For the first time in your whole life you felt alive, you felt loved and seen and safe. Then one day, you got scared and realised that what you are doing will not be approved by anyone around you. So you decided to go back to your comfortable life. To the life you knew so well. The life which will never hurt or surprise you.

You are not quite sure however, if that spark, satisfied for now, will ever again start burning you from the inside, probably even stronger than before because it now knows the taste of real love, the love you were born to feel and live."

"Alex, that is not fair." For the first time, Alex saw tears in Noelle's eyes. She stopped herself. She knew she probably pushed too hard. The truth sometimes hurts. It hurts deep and now they both felt that pain. A pain Alex carried around her since their conversation over the phone, a conversation which unexpectedly dimmed their light and put a question mark on their so far perfect relationship.

Once they shared such a strong desire and deep love now pain was their common ground. Their language. "You don't understand."

"But, Noelle, I do," Alex continued a little bit softer. "I understand exactly what you are going through. I always have. I was there 15 years ago myself. Discovering who I was, questioning everything I knew, feeling like I will disappoint everyone I love.

Feeling condemned for the feelings I felt. Doomed and sentenced without a trial. I thought I will never possibly be able to even try and be myself. I didn't know who myself was. So I packed my bags and left. I started fresh in this city and life was never better.

Everything started to make sense and every experience brought me closer to who I was meant to be. To who I am right now. Of course I understand how hard it is for you, how lost you must feel and also how relieved you must have felt once you finally let yourself be, well you.

That's why I never pushed you, I never demanded or asked you to do anything you were not comfortable with. I never asked you to change your life, I just let you do what you thought was best. You planned, you made decisions you promised me things you could not deliver."

"I am sorry." Noelle didn't know what to say. All that Alex said was true, all the actions were hers, so were the decisions and promises she made. The truth, however, didn't make it any easier.

"It's OK." Few tears showed up on Alex's face. "See I understand, I always have. The problem is you don't understand the pain you have caused me. The pain of your broken promises, the future we were going to share together. All I ever did was love you and trust you."

"Alex, I still love you. I don't want things to change between us." Noelle's words seemed empty just like her promises.

"And how do you think this is going to work? Do I get Tuesday, Thursday and every other weekend?" Alex was trying to bring some humour into the conversation. She knew her next best move is to walk away and give Noelle the space she needed. Easier said than done when love for someone is still burning bright inside your every cell.

"I guess that could work."

"It could," Alex smiled. "I am not that person Noelle, I am better than being someone's bit on the side, even if that someone is you."

"What are you saying?" Now Noelle seemed confused, she wasn't used to people refusing her offers.

"What I am saying is that you have a decision to make. If you want me, it has to be all in. Not just when it is convenient for you, not anymore."

"Can we see each other again? Can we not just finish it like this?"

"Noelle, I have given you months now to figure out what and how you want it. I was patient until you told me you are not leaving your husband. What would that make me if I still kept seeing you?"

"Nothing has to change."

"But everything did. What would happen if you make plans with me but Liam needs something. How would that make me feel if you had to change your plans to prioritise your marriage? Or if he finds out about us? You will have to make a choice then and just drop me, just like that overnight.

"Do you know what that would do to my soul? I need to protect myself, Noelle. I need to protect myself from this and keep whatever morality I have left. I thought you weren't happy. I thought you were going to leave your husband either way. I never thought I was just a chapter in your life, a mid-life crisis perhaps."

"But you are more than that, you know what I feel for you is real, it is strong and it is pure."

"Yet it is not enough, and maybe it will never be enough." Alex wiped a tear from her eye. "But that is OK. Focus on how much this relationship has given us, how much we learned from each other and the good times we had. And who knows maybe it's not a good bye."

"What are we going to do? We will see each other in the office. I can't just pretend I don't have feelings for you."

"It's OK." Alex made some decisions already, decisions that will make it easier. "I will go back to Poland and oversee the new Head office. I will make sure all is done and dusted and all the operations are up to standards, that should take what 2-3 months. That will give us both time to figure out what's best."

"I don't want not to see you. I don't think I can just stop seeing you for 2-3 months? Alex, I don't think I can handle that."

"See, Noelle, this is where the problem is; it's all about what you want. You never once thought of what I need to get over this. What I need to make a peace with our future just falling apart because of your choices."

"You need to be away from me?" Noelle started to get it.

"I can't see you and not want to hold you or kiss you. I can't be close to you and not want you to come back to my place so I can taste you again."

"I understand. So when are you going?"

"Probably in a week or two. I might go away first to Spain maybe for a week. Take some time to think before going back to work."

"It's probably for the best." Noelle closed her eyes and took a deep breath. "It pains me you know. I just don't know how I can make it all work, how I can make everyone happy."

"But you should not worry about that, your only job in life is to make yourself happy."

"I have responsibilities, Alex."

"Noelle, your only responsibility is towards your kids, and being a happy, fulfilled mother will give them more happiness than being a mother who will always question her choices. So take this time and make a choice you won't regret later. I am here to support and help you but I also need to look after myself."

"Thank you," Noelle whispered and gave Alex a long, tight hug. "Thank you, Alex, for your love and understanding, and I really hope this is not the end."

"That is completely up to you," Alex replied with a heavy heart.

Katy

The night finally came where Katy was able to show off her party planning and organisational skills. She got a permission from Noelle to organise a party in the office celebrating recent success and a deep budget. Decorations covered every wall and the large meeting room, catering with sushi and finger food was ordered, and arriving any minute she even got a DJ and a small inflatable bar.

What she was most proud of was however the arrangement of champagne glasses in a pyramid. She was going to start pouring the goods once everyone Is here. She was proud of her work and waited for both Noelle and Alex with anticipation.

She knew Alex likes certain signers so arranged a full album or two of Ariana Grande to be played sporadically threw the night. She thought Alex will appreciate the extra touch, after all the recent success was mostly thanks to her. She even picked up the heavy lifting when Noelle had to stay home with her kids. She was sure Noelle will appreciate all the extra effort Katy went to in order to show Alex their gratitude.

The party was slowly starting, everyone arrived on time, quite unusual she thought. She started pouring bottles and bottles of champagne to fill up all of the glasses in her genius construction. Noelle made a toast, so did Alex after and everyone started mingling in celebration. Katy tried to find Alex in the small office crowd which wasn't hard.

What was hard was to get her alone in amidst of all the people who wanted to talk to her and congratulate her. Not to mention Noelle, she seemed to be holding Alex in her firm grasp all night. No wonder she was her new gold start, a high achiever and the next few months in Poland were quite important, and Alex was happy to take it all on her own.

She was hard working and well admired not only in this office but also other branches. Katy wondered if Alex will ever come back to work here or will she try to expand other markets or find a different part of the business. She was flying out next week and the thought of not seeing Alex for a while was bringing a feeling of sadness.

Katy didn't want to miss this opportunity, it was about 10:30 and she knew Alex won't be staying much longer. She finally noticed Alex on her own walking towards the jackets. She had to take this chance and talk to her.

Alex

Alex came to the office party against her better judgement. It seemed to her this was something she has done regularly of late. She knew all the hard work Katy put into organising this and for how long she was trying to convince both her and Noelle that a success of this calibre needs a suitable celebration. She came not to disappoint Katy but didn't plan on staying long.

The effort put into it was truly impressive. She enjoyed the champagne display and had to keep her professionalism and cool head and give a little speech after Noelle's. She was trying to keep her distance from her and engage in as many conversations with other colleagues as possibly. After all, there was not much they could say to each other. Everything was very raw, just painfully bubbling at top of the surface.

Every look in Noelle's direction previously bringing so much peace and hope, was now just a reminder of what could have been, in some way what she lost. To make matters worse, the DJ seemed to be a big fan of Ariana Grande. All of the songs previously like a background to her relationship with Noelle were now forcing her to reminisce every night out they had together; every moment they spend wrapped in Alex's sheets form that first time in a hotel one afternoon to the last night they shared in her apartment.

That night they went out to celebrate their relationship. She never thought it would be the last time she can hold Noelle in her arms. She looked at Noelle through a crowd of heads and Noelle looked at her at the same time. Their eyes met and the feeling of pain escalated in her heart. She thought she can handle it until she heard the lyrics of the song playing in the background…

The whole playlist of today's evening was like a soundtrack to her relationship with Noelle. From "I'm so into you", "Break Free" to "Love me harder", Ariana Grande's voice and most of all words were like little daggers in Alex's heart. She tried her best not to break out in tears in front of all the guests, she held herself together the best she could until the chores came on. Ironically, she too wanted to break free, from this party, from those memories. She swiftly made her way to the bathroom where she hoped to be alone. She stood in front of the mirror as if trying to pick up the broken pieces of her heart when the door opened. Noelle walked in wearing a tight black dress, her hair up high and long gold earrings complementing her look.

She gently closed the door behind her, turned the lock and threw herself towards Alex. She took her face with both hands and started kissing her passionately. She finally looked at Alex and whispered, "I don't want this to end, not like this".

It seemed the music was making them both not just remember but crave what they were willingly walking away from.

"Let's get out of here please."

"Out of this bathroom?" Alex wasn't sure what Noelle wants.

"No, silly out of this office. Let's go to the club or one of our pubs and talk I want to be with you tonight and only you. I can't handle all of these people around you."

"I will walk out first and get my jacket, I will meet you outside in 10 minutes." Alex didn't know what Noelle want's at this point she didn't know what she wanted either.

One moment she felt as if her world was falling apart and now there is a glimmer of hope. Did Noelle change her mind? Is she not willing to give this up? She didn't want to feel any more hurt but she couldn't walk away without hearing her out.

Alex opened the bathroom door and made sure there is no one around before she walked out. She made her way towards the jackets and was hoping she can slip out unsees when she heard a voice behind her.

"Alex, I was waiting to talk to you all night. Are you enjoying the party?" Katy was happy to finally get her on her own.

"Oh, Hi," Alex realised she didn't talk to her today, she was nervously looking towards the bathroom door.

"Are you going home already?" Katy seemed disappointed.

"I'm sorry. The party is great, you have done a great job. I just have a little bit of a headache I can't shift all day." Alex tried her best not to raise any suspicion.

"Alex," Katy put her hand on Alex's arm. "I know this isn't the right time but I don't know when is. I was holding it back in Poland as I know you were so busy, but now you are going away again and I don't know when I am going to see you. I feel like you need to…" She was blushing, Alex wasn't sure what was going on she was still nervously glancing behind them. She looked at Katy with a confused look.

"I don't know how to even say it; in my mind it was much smoother," Katy continued. "I think you are really great." She gave Alex a kiss on the cheek.

"Oh, Katy, I'm sorry. I think you are really great too but more like a little sister kind of way." The same moment she was letting Katy's advances down Noelle walked out of the bathroom. She walked past them and gave them a little smile.

Alex couldn't help but look at her with a hunger in her eyes. She was trying not to seem distracted and looked back at Katy.

"I understand," Katy whispered. "I am so sorry I should have never."

"No it's OK, are you OK?" Alex wanted to make sure she is fine before she went chasing after her ice queen.

"I'm fine," Katy smiled. She looked a little embarrassed. "Alex, be careful."

"What do you mean?" Alex was afraid Katy noticed the looks between them, she wasn't sure what she meant however.

"With Noelle." Katy didn't want to stick a nose in their business but she was obviously worried for Alex.

"There is," Alex was trying to deny anything happening but she didn't even bother. "What do you mean by be careful." The curiosity was stronger than the want to defend Noelle's honour.

"Look, Alex, I really like you. Noelle is my boss and she is a great one. I just don't want you to get hurt."

"Is there a reason why I might?" Alex wished they had this conversation months ago, it was a little too late now.

"Please don't tell Noelle I told you this, mostly it's just office gossip you know. Well some of it anyway." Alex nodded her head in agreement. "There was this guy here years ago. Him and Noelle worked on a thing together and everyone could see he sort of got obsessed with her; it seemed she was enjoying it too.

"Until it went too far, he left his wife and two kids. In the end, he showed up in her house. They had to get a restraining order. HR looked into it and there was nothing Noelle did so, he just went crazy, some say from the unfulfilled desire for her."

"OK." Alex was surprised. "Seems like Noelle didn't do anything wrong?"

"That's not all," Katy continued. "There was an intern here last summer, Daniel or Damian, I can't really remember his name. She send him some pictures and emails. Sort of border line inappropriate."

"How did that end?" Alex was feeling sick.

"He showed them to me." Katy felt embarrassed but she was glad she shared this with Alex. She liked Alex and didn't want anything upsetting happening to her.

"What did the emails say?" Alex wanted to know more.

"Ah they were just of an overly flirtatious nature. See he was gay and felt really uncomfortable. I asked him to ignore it, he was leaving shortly anyway. He promised not to say anything."

"So you covered for her?" Alex wasn't sure what to say or how to react.

"Sort of I guess. He left just a few weeks before you started. She does that sometimes, Alex. She likes when people get attached to her, she showers them with attention and sort of special treatment until they are kind of obsessed I guess and then just takes a step back. Leaves them craving for more."

"Thank you, Katy." Alex felt her stomach turning around. "I really appreciate your honesty and I will never say anything. I need to go now."

Alex ran back into the toilet and once again the feeling of crushing pain was so strong the content of her stomach emptied out nearly immediately. She felt played, she felt used, she felt stupid. How can she look Noelle in the eyes and listen to what she has to say after this.

Was she just a toy? Just another office fling or some sort of game, someone's entertainment. She didn't want to believe that, she couldn't believe that. She remembered Noelle mentioned that a few times she found herself flirting with people and then she would feel guilty, that she was looking for something and wasn't sure what it is she is looking for. Until she met Alex.

She had to believe she was more than another time passing chapter in her bosses chase for fulfilment. She saw it in her eyes. She saw it in the way her body reacted to Alex's touch. Alex washed her face and made herself look as normal as possible.

She had to face Noelle and see what she has to say. She had to pretend everything is OK and she didn't just hear these soul destroying news. She put on her best poker face and walked out of the bathroom towards the jackets, this time without the patience to talk to anyone in her path.

She took her jacket and headed for the entrance when she heard the lyrics of the next song, Miley Cyrus's raspy voice was expressing exactly what she felt. She walked towards the door with "Nothing breaks like a heart" teasing her from the speaker.

How extremely fucking accurate, she thought to herself. She opened the door leaving the party, thrown to celebrate her success behind.

Noelle

Noelle was getting inpatient. She was waiting outside of the office building for about 20 minutes now. She didn't want to text Alex, she felt she was walking on thin ice as it is so didn't want to add any pressure. She was sure Alex was doing her best to get out as quick as she can.

The last thing Noelle saw when she was leaving was Alex talking to Katy, she was sure she will be able to finish that conversation soon. Unless…no Katy wouldn't do that, she wouldn't betray her and release any of her secrets. Noelle brushed off the thought as soon as it came. Finally, the door opened and to her delight it was indeed Alex.

They walked to the pub, it was only a couple of streets away and the town was busy so getting a taxi would probably take longer. They didn't talk much on the way. Noelle didn't know how to start and Alex didn't seem in the mood for a trivial conversation. Noelle took Alex's hand however, and Alex didn't protest.

It gave Noelle some hope that maybe not all is lost. They walked into what they once thought of as 'their' pub and found an empty table. It was facing a window but at this time all of the windows were covered with dark blinds.

Alex went to the bar and ordered two glasses of prosecco and some water to clear her throat. Noelle tried to kiss her when she came back to the table, Alex however, moved her head and she was only able to catch the side of her cheek.

"Are you OK?" Noelle asked finally.

"Sure," Alex nodded. "And you?"

"I missed you." Noelle touched Alex's hand gently, Alex closed her eyes. She leaned in again and Alex didn't move this time. They kissed. For Alex, it was both pleasure and pain.

"What are we doing here?" Alex asked. It seemed she was running out of patience, something she normally had in abundance.

"I just wanted to see you, before you go to Poland."

"You can see me in the office."

"Not like this."

"And what is this?" Alex was tired of playing games, she wanted to know what she stands on.

"I might be able to come to Poland maybe next month? Would you like that?"

"It's your company, your big break. I think it doesn't matter what I would like." Alex wanted answers not empty promises. Noelle could feel how displeased she was.

"Alex, I want to come to see you. To be with you."

"And what are you going to tell your husband?"

"That's fair." Noelle moved back. She understood Alex was not going to play ball. Not by those rules. "I still have very strong feelings for you."

"And yet you still sleep in the same bed as the man you married."

"You know it's complicated."

"Noelle," Alex looked at Noelle as if to give it her last shot. "You say you love me, you want to be with me, you kiss me when no one sees, you are here with me drinking and I don't know what we are even doing. You want to come to Poland soon?"

"Yes, I would love that," Noelle jumped in eagerly.

"All we have is now. Why wait to be together on someone's stolen time in Poland in the future, come home with me now? If you really want me."

"You know I can't, not like this." Noelle was getting agitated, Alex was breaking all the boundaries she once set. As if she was no longer under her spell.

In that moment, Alex realised Noelle wants to keep her close. She wants to keep her just close enough to have her in her grasp but isn't willing to either commit or change her life. Perhaps, she will never be able to leave her life regardless of what she says.

Alex had to harvest all the strength and will power she had left. She looked at Noelle, she still loved her however that love was now causing her so much pain and suffering.

"Remember when you told me once that you can no longer live a lie? That your eyes have now been opened? It was that afternoon in the park, you touched me and told me you loved me for the first time. And now you chose to throw this all away for what?

"It doesn't matter if a lie consists of a picture-perfect life, it is still a lie. A lie you are willingly choosing to live. I have nothing to say to you, Noelle. Not until you either decide to stay with your husband or go after what you really want.

What your heart desires. I will be on a plane next week and I would like for us to take a break from communication. Please respect that. I need this to get over, well you."

Alex smiled and gave Noelle a kiss on the forehead. With all the pain, she was still soft and loving.

"Take care and look after yourself." Alex stood up and walked out of the pub. Noelle followed a while later. She got into the taxi and cried. She got home and was thankful everyone was still asleep. She knew she had a decision to make but over the next few months, she will leave Alex to focus on work.

She didn't want to hurt her any longer and wanted to respect Alex's wish until she was able to make some decisions. It was only fair for both of them. She felt as much pain as Alex did. She was torn between and known and the unknown. The old and the new, the commitment and desire.

As always, she felt she needs to be so many things for so many people; how was she ever going to make the right choice and not regret it later. She decided to spend the next few months trying to appreciate what she has. Maybe that will bring some clarity.

Alex

Alex took a glass of white wine and went up to the roof top with a new book. She enjoyed the last few weeks since coming back from Poland. It was calm and peaceful and once she made decisions regarding Noelle; she was able to start the healing.

It's been a couple of months and not seeing her was the best decision she made. She knew she can't heal while still being in her company. She started dating again, she also discovered how to enjoy her alone time. More than anything.

Alex was consumed by the book when the door to the roof terrace opened. It was a communal space but to her delight there was hardly anyone there. She noticed her glass is empty, she will have to go down to fill it up. It was approaching 8, so the door will soon be locked anyway.

As she stood up, she saw a figure on the other side, taking pictures of the sun setting in the horizon. It did indeed give the river an unusual, pink, and purple shimmer. It was beautiful. So was the woman taking the pictures. Alex knew her name is Karina.

She saw her around so many times and heard the tragic love story from Gabriela. She was somehow intrigued and curious about his woman. She approached her slowly as if she was walking towards a wild animal; she didn't want to startle or disrupt the moment.

"Your glass seems empty," Karina pointed sharply.

"It is, indeed, I'm Alex," she smoothly used the situation to introduce herself.

"I'm Karina," Karina smiled. "I must apologies for being so…"

"Observative," Alex interrupted. "It's OK, that's how you make a living." She was sharp and witty, trades most really liked but only some didn't fear.

"A fan of my work?" Karina asked playfully.

"I can't say that I have seen any, but I'm opened to being enlightened." Alex was charming and smooth.

"Well, how about you let me top up that glass first." Karina could easily match that.

"The night is young, why not."

They walked out of the terrace together and got into the elevator. Karina opened a bottle of white wine as soon as they got into her apartment and poured them both a glass. Alex noticed pictures lying on the island in the middle of the kitchen.

"May I?" She asked. As she was approaching, she noticed a picture of Gabriela, covered in silky sheets, asleep. It made her feel uneasy; she took as step back realising it was private and not for anyone to see.

"I would rather if you didn't. I'm sorry I didn't expect company. I just developed them; they were taken a long time ago."

"It's OK." Alex smiled which brought comfort to Karina. "You don't have to explain we all have a past; we all keep little souvenirs of that past. Here," she put her hand on her heart. "Or in something more tangible," she pointed at the pictures.

"What about the 'what might have been'?" Karina asked. "Where do we keep those?" She was curious as to what Alex's reply will be. She took a moment before she shared her opinion.

"I don't think many of us realise there is no such thing as what might have been. We have one chance in life, at anything really but especially at well people," she smiled.

"If you want something, if you want her bad, nothing will stop you from trying. There is no such thing as circumstances or timing, it's just a story we tell ourselves to make excuses for our own inability to change our life, to take control to take risks." She took a sip of wine before she continued.

"Whatever was, it is all that would ever have been, it was all that we were supposed to experience with that person. Turn the what if into thank you, be grateful for what you had and for the lesson it taught you. We need to change the narrative from, the one forever to the one for now. Whatever you have had or experienced it was the right thing for you at the time, but that all it was."

"Cheers to that!" Karina was impressed and more intrigued by Alex. "Well said, miss Alex." She smiled and walked towards Alex to clink their glasses.

"Well, thank you," Alex was flattered, she felt like she passed some sort of a test.

They walked out to the balcony and sat for a couple of hours, they talked and shared ideas. They chatted about nature, grounding, romance, women, and food. They talked about everything and nothing at the same time. It was easy, free flowing and comfortable.

Something Karina didn't experience much, normally people would feel on edge with her, somehow intimidated, Alex however, was different. Such confidence was rare.

"Oh god, it's after getting late." Alex looked at her watch, midnight was approaching. She didn't want to overstay.

"Will you turn into a pumpkin?" Karina laughed.

"Something like that," Alex replied. "Thank you for well the wine, good company, and a great conversation, I think I needed it." She continued with a smile on her face. They came into the living room leaving the cold April night behind them.

Alex walked towards the door. She had a lovely time and was going to try and see Karina again. Just to share another exciting conversation, she felt comfortable in her company, and she enjoyed not knowing where the chat will bring them next time.

"Thank you for the wine," she said gratefully. "I'm sure I will see you again soon," she added more as a matter of fact than a question. Karina did something she didn't expect herself to do. She walked towards Alex and grabbed her by the collar of her Polo T-shirt, she pulled her body towards hers and kissed her.

Alex didn't flinch, she kissed her back with confidence and calmness. Something Karina was not used to. She never met anyone with such a peace inside and beautiful quiet confidence outside. It was both exciting and scary.

She was afraid she might lose control, ironically this is something she wanted all along. Alex looked Karina in the eyes, those almond shaped, black eyes so many have drawn in. She felt a pull towards Karina from the moment she saw her months ago, but she didn't want to do anything too quickly. She didn't want this to be just a one-night stand or a chain of uncomfortable encounters.

"Come over to my place tomorrow," Alex whispered. "I owe you some wine and a good conversation."

"I would like that." Karina smiled a shy, cute smile no one has ever seen before.

"How's 8 working for you?" She asked without hesitation.

"Eight is perfect," Alex responded, she kissed Karina's hand and swiftly left her apartment.

Karina found herself 30 minutes later, standing with her back to the door. She was thinking about Alex, about her lips on her lips, those strong arms, brown eyes, and dimples. What was it about this girl, this woman was different than all the others?

She couldn't figure that one out just yet, she was however intrigued. She looked forward to tomorrow she didn't know what the night might bring.

Karina

She must have changed her outfit about 5 times. She wanted something casual, but also sexy. She wasn't sure why she is trying so hard to impress someone, she was normally the one people were trying to impress. She put on jeans and a shirt, it was perfect for a drink with a neighbour, comfortable, smart, and casual.

She picked a nice bottle of wine and a fruit basket from nearby organic market and was ready to rock to Alex's door by 8 pm. She knocked.

"Hi." Alex opened the door in black, tight jeans, and a black shirt tucket in into her jeans, tight on her body, perfectly complementing her athletic frame.

"Hi," Karina answered.

"Come in," Alex smiled, her dimples showing like a secret weapon, paralysing anyone who got close enough, like a venom of charm.

"Here, this is for you," Karina handed the wine and fruit.

"Well, thank you," Alex seemed surprised by the generosity. "That's sweet, I didn't take you for a sweet type." She laughed, somehow, she could get away with anything she said, even if it was borderline cheeky.

"Well, what type did you take me for?" Karina was well able for her.

"I guess I shouldn't judge the book by its cover." She came up with a quick and witty reply.

"I guess you shouldn't."

Karina walked in and they both sat around the kitchen table, Alex made dinner. A nice and light pasta with tomatoes, basil, and feta cheese. It was bubbling happily in the oven. They started the bottle of wine and sat very close to each other.

They only spoke once before but some invisible power was pulling them towards each other. They coud both feel the tension and were trying to do their best not to come across too eager, too excited, they also both enjoyed the anticipation. They lasted 20 minutes before their lips met again, and for the last 10, they couldn't even focus on the words coming out of their mouth.

They sat closer to each other; their knees bumped together a few times. They looked into each other's eyes and that was game over, for both. Karina tilted her head, Alex moved closer responding to her body language. They kissed; they both felt the fireworks you read about in stories.

Their hearts beat stronger, louder, their breath became short and sharp. Karina sat on top of Alex and started to unbutton her shirt, slowly, she liked to taker her time. She continued to kiss Alex as her hands swiftly worked their way down. She took off Alex's bra and took in the view. She enjoyed what she was seeing.

"You have a beautiful body Alex," she whispered in her ear.

Alex stood up, she lifted Karina effortlessly. She carried her to the bedroom and gently placed her on the bed. She took off Karina's top, she wasn't wearing a bra and she didn't need one. Her breasts were perfect, bouncy, round, the kind people pay for.

Her skin was the colour of caramel. It was beautiful, and the smell. A musky but light smell covered Karina's whole body, from her hair all the way to her feet. Alex was intrigued and excited to uncover all of Karina's secrets. She looked into Karina's eyes while she slowly opened her jeans, she started slipping them off.

They both were impatient at his point. Alex continued to kiss Karina and lick her skin, bite her ear, she looked into her eyes as she slipped her finger inside her. Karina felt as if she was doing it for the first time, as if she was having sex for the first time in her life. This was different and they both knew it was somehow special. To her own surprise Karina came quickly. Alex was still kissing her, and the moment seemed to have last forever.

They looked into each other's eyes and Karina felt as if Alex can see right thought her soul. She didn't want to let that go, not for now anyway. Alex wasn't finished, she wasn't selfish that's for sure. She wanted to pleasure Karina for as long as she could. She was fascinated by her body, by how smooth it was, her scent, her skin, all of it.

She gently turned her around, she continued kissing her neck while her hands gently run up and down, once again she slipped her fingers inside this time from the back.

"You can play," she whispered into Karina's ear. "You can do what you like."

Karina felt comfortable with Alex, despite the fact they only knew each other for a couple of days. She did what she wouldn't do with any other stranger. She reached down and pleasured herself. She enjoyed what Alex was doing to her body and once again she gave in completely.

She let go of control and let herself feel. She got lost with this beautiful stranger. After they were finished, they lied in each other's arms, just taking in the moment, and enjoying the company, Karina looked at Alex.

"You are different," she told her.

"Am I now?" Alex laughed; deep down she knew.

"I think it's your turn now," Karina whispered seductively, biting Alex's ear.

It was her playground now, Alex was hers. She run her tongue around Alex's nipples, she bit them slightly, she licked her stomach, kissed the insights of her thighs. She looked at Alex, her eyes were closed. Karina smiled. She put her tongue between Alex's legs and could hear Alex moan.

She was now in control and Alex was hers to do with what she wanted. She was going to take her for a ride, she was going to make her beg. She played until she felt Alex was close to a finish line; she stopped then and slipped her fingers inside Alex. Once again she brought her tongue between Alex's legs and was now pleasuring her in two ways.

Alex's body arched and every muscle got very tight, she was pushing Karina's head down, she liked it. No one ever had enough courage to do that, her other hand was holding a firm grasp around the sheets.

Once again Alex was close to a climax and Karina stopped, the look at Alex's face, it was a mix of confusion, frustration, and pleasure.

"Get up," Karina ordered, and Alex followed.

She got down on her knees and started eating Alex out, she pushed one of her legs up and put her fingers inside. This time she was going to let her finish, she wasn't going to be that cruel. It didn't take long. Alex possibly experienced the most intense orgasm in her life.

To the point she squirted all over the sheets. Something she at first felt very embarrassed about.

Karina and Alex

The morning Sun sneaked in through the blinds casting its spell over the room, Karina woke up to find a note next to the bed.

> 'Went out for coffee, be back soon.'

She read the note with a smile and got up to open the blinds to fully let the sun spread across the room and her naked body. She took the blanket and went out to the balcony to feel the breeze and enjoy this morning in all its glory. And what a glorious morning it was.

The clouds moved slowly, pushed by the subtle bursts of wind. Sun peaked through them anywhere it could, and its rays bounced of the calm water. Birds flying playfully chirping in the distance. Karina closed her eyes and took a deep breath.

The sun warming up her skin made the morning cool breeze a little warmer. Consumed with this moment and a memory of last night, she didn't hear Alex coming back into the apartment. It also took her awhile to realise she stayed over. Something she has never done before.

For some reason it didn't scare her, she was at ease, she was happy and content. A feeling quite foreign was now bringing ease to her existence. Alex came into the room with a large tray, fresh fruit, warm bagels, and a smell of coffee that filled the room. Karina walked back into the bedroom closing the balcony door behind her.

"Good morning," Alex greeted her playfully. She was effortless in everything she did.

"Hey." Karina smiled, she sat on the bed and picked up a cup of coffee.

"How are you feeling?" Alex asked caringly, her kindness and tenderness was a complete opposite to what she was like in bed. Strong, firm, dominating. Karina never met anyone quite like her.

"How do you think I'm feeling?" She threw the ball back into Alex's corner as she took a bite of a still warm bagel with peanut butter and jam. "That's very sophisticated," she laughed pointing at the breakfast.

"Sophisticated or not, it's nutritious and will help you restore your energy." Alex's face was covered with that cheeky, dirty smile.

"And what do I need that energy for?" Karina asked playfully knowing well what the day had in store.

They hardly left the bed, maybe just to get a glass of water to replenish some lost fluids. Their energy was matched on all levels, the conversation, the curiosity and openness towards life and their passion and compatibility was out of this world. Nothing either of them has ever experienced.

"You know I was never in love before," Karina shared with Alex at some point during the day.

"Isn't that nice." The answer was confusing.

"What do you mean?" Karina followed up.

"I will be your first." Alex smiled and kissed Karina before she was able to blur out a reply. Deep down, Karina was afraid she might be right. She was afraid something was changing, and she wasn't sure she was ready for a change.

"So," Karina gave Alex a serious look. "You are not going to plan our wedding now, are you?" She was trying to keep it light, but those conversations never ended well.

"Nah," Alex seemed unbothered. "I will leave the details for you."

"I'm serious, Alex." Karina stood up and lit a cigarette out on the balcony. "Do we need to have the talk?" She asked.

"We don't need to do anything," Alex was cool about whatever Karina wanted to discuss.

"You know I just date around," Karina kept going.

"Sure." Alex understood what she meant. She wasn't sure how she feels about it, but it was too early to make any demands or ask Karina to make any changes in her life. She was just enjoying what they had. She knew she will develop feelings for this amazing, beautiful woman and she needed to be gentle with herself, she didn't want to end up with a broken heart, not again.

"So," Karina continued. "You wouldn't be upset if I fucked someone else? I think I want to keep seeing you, but I can't commit. I don't do relationships." Alex took a deep long breath, as if she was weighing her words carefully. She smiled.

"I will give you two weeks and we can talk again then."

Karina was both slightly shocked but impressed by her response. Alex had balls and wasn't afraid to speak her mind. At the end of the day, she knew what she had to offer, and she wasn't afraid to put all the cards on the table.

Alex on the other side, knew her limitations and she knew she can't be OK with Karina seeing other people once she falls for her. She wanted to avoid that at all costs.

Karina stayed over another night and went home the following morning. She had to travel to Belfast for a couple of days, a trip she planned few weeks before. She also had some friends she wanted to visit so she would stay an extra night.

To her surprise she was thinking about Alex. She was texting her the whole way down.

Noelle

It had been 4 months since Noelle last saw Alex. They agreed not to reach out to each other, not to see each other. It was hard at first but with time Noelle got back into her routine. She respected Alex's boundaries and was hoping what she felt for her will fade away.

Four months later, however, the memory of Alex might have been fading but the love and passion she once felt was still burning inside of her. She needed to see her, she wanted to keep Alex in her life in any capacity she could. Was she able to change her life? To leave her life, if Alex was to take her back maybe one day, she will have enough courage to do so.

She took out her phone and checked her messages. She reached out to Alex the day before and to her surprise Alex agreed to meet her. She felt excited, a little scared even. Will they be able to talk to each other as easily as before? Will she still see the same beauty in Alex's face?

She wanted to find answers to those questions sooner rather than later. She missed her, she missed how her hair felt on her skin, she missed her smell and her touch. Most of all she missed how safe and at peace she felt in Alex's company. She missed who she was with her. Who Alex allowed her to be.

Noelle spent a better part of an hour trying to find the perfect clothes. She picked tight, grey suit pants and cashmere jumper; it complemented her long blond hair. Liam took the boys away for the weekend with his parents which gave her a perfect opportunity to meet Alex. Maybe even to spend some more time with her.

She didn't know where the coffee is going to take them, she was hopeful, nonetheless. She took a taxi to town, so she doesn't have to worry about the car. Maybe they will go out for a drink after the coffee? Who knows? What she wouldn't give to feel the excitement of being out with Alex again.

Noelle visited their favourite bar a couple of times, she felt at ease there. She felt like she belonged to something bigger than herself, she felt like she had a community. Without Alex however it wasn't the same. Maybe today she will be able to get back a glimpse of what it was like, a taste.

All she wanted is a little reminder. A little window into what could have been or maybe into what will be. The taxi arrived in town and dropped her outside their coffee shop. So many memories, so much pleasure and pain, Noelle felt a bittersweet feeling walking in.

"Running late, will be there in 5."

A text from Alex hit her phone. Her heart started beating faster. She was glad Alex was late, that will give her a chance to get settled and collect her thoughts. She ordered a soya latte, americano with coconut milk and a Vegan peanut butter square. She smiled thinking about the times where this was their regular breakfast.

She took the tray upstairs and to her delight only two other people were enjoying their Saturday coffee, most importantly 'their' seat was free. She put the tray down, took of her coat and gently placed it on the armchair. She sat on 'her' side of the coach and fixed her hair. She wanted to look perfect, she wanted this to be perfect.

She took a sip of her coffee as a shadow emerged from the door. It was Alex. Noelle's heart started beating even stronger, she found it hard to catch a breath and the palms of her hands started to sweat. Just like the first time they kissed…

Alex

Alex didn't expect the text message from Noelle. She contemplated reaching out to her a couple of times, just to check in, make sure she is doing OK but each time she stopped herself. She set the boundaries and Noelle respected them and she felt it would have been hypocritical to break them.

She was glad to hear from her and was looking forward to catching up. It felt like meeting an old friend. Someone who once very dear to her heart, was now a reminder of the vast and long journey she has taken in her life. It's meeting Noelle that pushed her to taking all the steps that followed.

She took control of her life, left a relationship which wasn't working and realised her own worth. It's through Noelle's eyes she rediscovered herself again and it pushed her towards the direction she always wanted to go in life. She was happy with or without Noelle in her life, she was grateful for what they once had and made peace with the fact it was never going to be anything more.

Alex was happy she gets to see her however, Noelle was a big part of her reinvention and rediscovery, and she wanted to make sure Noelle knows, she wanted to thank her. She arrived at the meeting place a few minutes late. Noelle was already upstairs. Alex walked up the stairs and saw Noelle on the couch once upon a time they used to treat like home.

She walked towards Noelle with a big smile on her face and kindness in her eyes. Something Noelle forgot about. They talked for ages about the last few months, what they have been up to. How Noelle's kids are. How Alex found working in the new office after coming back from Poland.

She asked for a transfer and Noelle never made an issue. Another thing Alex was grateful for. It must have been nearly two hours later when Alex looked at her watch.

"Should we go or would you like another coffee?" Alex asked not sure how long Noelle can stay. It seemed they spoke about everything they could, they were both happy to see each other and even happier to share how well they are both doing.

"Another coffee would be nice," Noelle replied. "Or maybe a drink?"

"A drink?" The rather bold ask amused Alex.

"Alex," Noelle looked down as if she was ashamed of what was going to come out of her mouth next. "I miss you, Alex."

"I missed you too, Noelle." Alex put her hand on Noelle's hand.

"No not that way. I miss your touch. I miss your smell. I miss being with you." Noelle looked at Alex. Alex closed her eyes processing the information she was hearing. Noelle leaned in and kissed Alex's lips, she lingered for a few seconds before Alex moved back.

"What are you doing?" Alex asked. She felt so many emotions racing through her body and mind.

"I want you back, it didn't feel right the last few months, not being able to see you or touch you." Noelle moved closer, she started playing with Alex's hair just like she used to in the past.

"Have you left your husband?" Alex's question came out sharp.

"No, of course I didn't." Noelle seemed surprised. She dropped her hair and moved back. She felt attacked.

"How can you tell me you want me back, Noelle, when you have not done anything to show me you are serious about us?"

"I am not strong enough without you, but one day I will be, I promise."

"So, you want me to just wait for that day? Sit at home every weekend, every Christmas, every new year, and any other occasion? Sit and wait till you are ready to finally make some changes and live your life?"

"Alex, where is this coming from? I don't have it all figured out, no one has. I just miss you and I was hoping that you miss me too, and maybe we can go and get a drink and talk. Remember like before."

"I remember, all too well. Noelle, you can't just come into someone's life and asked them to put it on hold just so you can figure things out; you had 4 months to do that. Four months to make decisions and changes. You can't just have it all. You can't just have a comfortable life with a loving and devoted husband and then have your fun on the side. Taking what you need from both of us and not really giving the same, fair amount of love or devotion back. How is that fair on either of us?"

"Alex, I understand you are upset. I know I have hurt you and I promise never to do that again. I want you in my life. I often think about how it would feel to live with you; how would it feel to wake up next to you; to fall asleep in your arms. I'm at home with my husband yes, but it is you I am thinking of that has not changed." Noelle moved closer to Alex again. She hoped her words will work.

"How can I believe you, Noelle? How can I believe that you won't go back on your promises again?"

"I guess all you can do is trust me." Noelle felt like she is gaining some ground. Was Alex going to give in? She wanted to kiss her so much. She wanted to go back to her place and feel her body on hers.

"I don't know if I can, Noelle, its better if I go. I need to think." Alex was confused and angry.

"Go, I understand." Noelle grabbed Alex's hand. "Just think how could you go through life never again feeling what we had? That special connection with someone you only read about in books. That passion? Can you really tell me you can walk away form that?

"Look me in the eyes and tell me you can chose to never feel my body against yours? Never feel my lips on your lips. Never feel that rush of blood into your head when we dance, when we fuck. Tell me you can make that choice?"

Alex looked at Noelle, thousand thoughts whirled through her mind like a hurricane. One thing was certain she cannot walk away from a connection she feels, a connection so perfect. A connection so strong it pulls you in and consumes you whole.

"I need a few days, Noelle," she pulled her hand and walked away.

"Take all the time you need." Noelle smiled, doing her best in trying to hide a hint of satisfaction.

Karina

"Ciao Bella." Adrianna's happy voice boomed on the other side of the phone.

"You are happy," Karina replied.

"How could I not be, life is beautiful, no?"

"I guess it is." Karina wasn't sharing her friend's enthusiasm.

"Oh no," Adrianna replied playfully. "What did you do?" She always seemed to know when Karina was in a bad form. The distance between them didn't matter she seemed to sense it straight away, a sign of real friendship.

"I didn't do anything." The accusation amused Karina.

"But you are not OK?" Adrianna continued the questioning.

"I met someone."

"OK."

"She's different, I don't know."

"And what did you do?"

"I didn't do anything, it's not like we are in a relationship. We literally just met."

"And yet whatever you did is not making you feel so good?"

"No, it is not, I have never felt like this," Karina continued. "We spent a weekend together and it was different, very easy. She is quite something. I was in Belfast this weekend. I went out and…"

"And you slept with someone?" Adrianna finished the sentence for her.

"Yes, but as soon as I did, it felt wrong. It didn't mean anything it was just a one-night stand. I have done it so many times before."

"But, Karina, my dear, sweet friend, you have never been in love before," Adrianna laughed.

"What do you mean?"

"What I mean is, you are falling for this girl, woman, and that is why being with someone else doesn't feel good or fulfilling. It feels wrong because she is not her."

"I hardly know Alex."

"That doesn't matter, I'm not saying you are in love with her, I'm saying you like her, a lot."

"I do," Karina took a long, deep breath. "So, what do I do now?"

"You have two options really, you either go on as you are and never see her again or you try to have a meaningful relationship and see where it takes you."

"What do you mean I don't see her again?"

"If you want to live your life like you had for the past 10 years, just going from one quick affair to the next, dating multiple people being whatever you call it, then you can't see this girl."

"Why?" Karina seemed confused.

"Because you don't want to hurt her, my dear," Adrianna continued. "You have broken enough hearts and you like this one, yes? So, spare her."

"So, I need to make a choice?"

"Ask yourself what you want to do. In my humble opinion, you either never see her again or you give it a try and stop seeing other people. Sure it doesn't even feel-good right?" Karina could feel Adriana smirk through the phone. "Your words."

"I hate you sometimes."

"I love you too," Adrianna replied playfully. "You good now?"

"Yes, I think I'm good." Karina wasn't sure. Her heart started saying one thing and her head was fighting to preserve the life she knew, the life that was so familiar and free from pain and disappointment. She always held all the cards, could she have changed after such a long time?

She never met anyone like Alex. She never felt guilty in a company of another woman.

"Call me next week to tell me what you have decided, OK." The warmth in Adrianna's voice was soothing.

"I will," Karina replied. "I promise."

"And Karina"

"Yes?"

"Don't be an idiot and don't lose her just because you are afraid of letting go and giving up some control. Sometimes it's nice not to always be in control, be brave, see what happens."

The call ended and it left Karina with more questions. Before the call she only felt guilt now the mix of emotions entered some new, unfamiliar ground. What she was going to do next was a mystery even to her.

Six Months Later...
Alex

Alex moved in with her girlfriend quite suddenly after they decided to make it official and exclusive. Against all odds, they both made changes in their life to give their relationship the best possible chance of making it work. They spent all their time together, so it only made sense to stay under the same roof.

She woke up early that morning and finally decided to start doing what she was always passionate about, she finally decided to start writing. She left her work as they both felt it will create a better balance for their new relationship. She took out her laptop and looked at the blank page, what she saw however, was a page full of possibilities waiting for her to pour her soul and inspiration.

It's something she always wanted to do. Writing was a part of her, and she finally had a story to tell and support to do what she wanted for so long. She started effortlessly, just like she has done anything in life. Anything came easy to her once she took control over her life and started listening to her inner voice.

'Dublin, a cosmopolitan city full of beautiful streets hiding secrets on every corner. A home to four women, despite different backgrounds, connected by the same desire for love and fulfilment. Through random encounters they embark on a journey to self-discovery which will change their lives forever.'

Characters:

Gabriela—a Brazilian student, quiet and calm girl looking for a new life and passionate love.

Karina—Persian strong and independent artist, withdrawn from human emotion.

Noelle—Mother, wife, businesswoman, caught up in her life and career not realising what she is missing is right in front of her.

Alex—Coming out of a long-time relationship believing life has more in store for her, doesn't want to settle for mediocre experiences, hungry for life.

Note—I will have to change the names.

Alex typed as a woman's voice came out of the bedroom.

"I'm going for a coffee run; do you want anything?"

"Can I have my regular?"

"Sure, americano with coconut milk it is," the woman's voice was closer. "Any pastries? Croissants?"

"Maybe a bagel," Alex smiled at the shadow coming out from behind the bedroom door.

"Bagel it is," she replied with a loving look in her eyes. "Alex, you are so beautiful." She approached Alex from behind, wrapped her arms around her and kissed her neck looking at the screen in front of them. "You started? I am so proud of you."

Alex turned around and put her arms around her partner. "I have," she whispered and kissed her plump lips.

"Withdrawn from human emotion," Karina laughed reading from the page. "Girl, that's harsh."

"Ah, you know, I have softened you." Alex smiled; she was the only one who could get away with this. Karina laughed and kissed Alex back.

"Yes, yes, you have. You put a spell on me. It's those dimples," Karina added as she headed for the door. "Back in 10; keep writing."

The door closed behind her, leaving Alex with a big smile on her face.

Note 2—I will definitely not change the ending.

The End